RICHARD SCRIMGER

INK ME

ORCA BOOK PUBLISHERS

Library and Archives Canada Cataloguing in Publication

Scrimger, Richard, 1957-
Ink me / Richard Scrimger.
(Seven (the series))

Issued also in an electronic format.
ISBN 978-1-4598-0016-8 (pbk.).—ISBN 978-1-4598-0017-5 (pdf).—
ISBN 978-1-4598-0018-2 (epub)

I. Title. II. Series: Seven the series
PS8587.C745I56 2012   jC813'.54   C2012-902625-5

First published in the United States, 2012
Library of Congress Control Number: 2012938313

Summary: Bunny goes to get a tattoo but inadvertently becomes involved with a gang.

MIX
Paper from
responsible sources
FSC® C016245
www.fsc.org

*Orca Book Publishers is dedicated to preserving the environment and has
printed this book on Forest Stewardship Council® certified paper.*

Orca Book Publishers gratefully acknowledges the support for its publishing
programs provided by the following agencies: the Government of Canada
through the Canada Book Fund and the Canada Council for the Arts,
and the Province of British Columbia through the BC Arts Council
and the Book Publishing Tax Credit.

Design by Teresa Bubela
Cover photography by Getty Images
Author photo by Brendan Humber

ORCA BOOK PUBLISHERS
www.orcabook.com

Printed and bound in Canada.

19 18 17 16 • 9 8 7 6

*To my mom, who may not have much time
for gang wars or tattoos but who loves kids
and books as much as anyone around.*

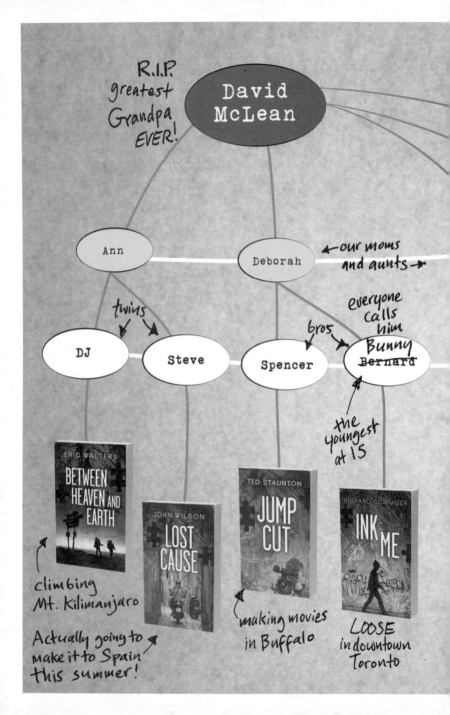

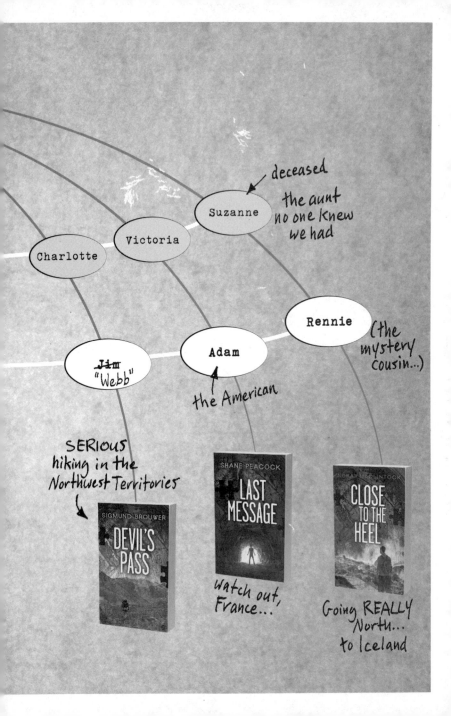

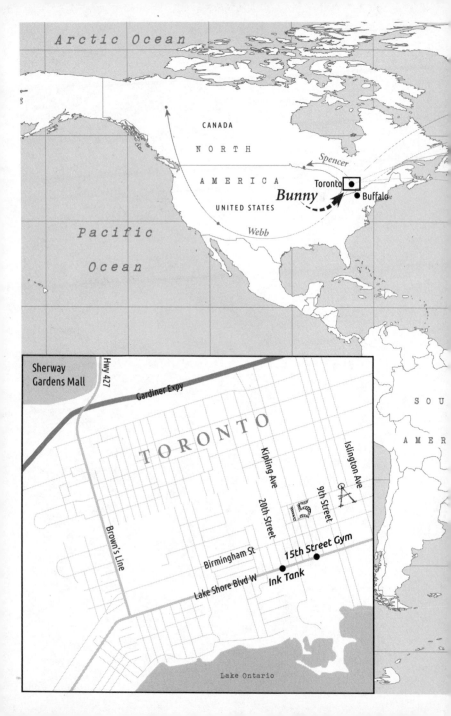

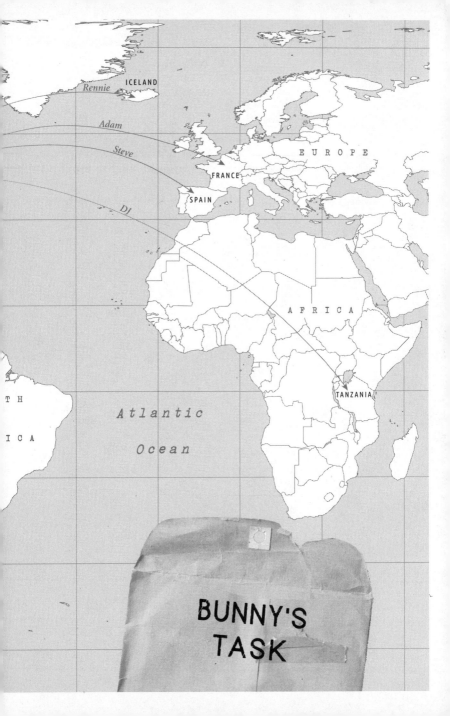

AFTER IT WAS OVER

SHE SAT ME DOWN at a big table and ast if
I wantd water or juice or anything.

No I said.

Or sum thing to eat—a bagel or muffin?

No.

My voys sounded funny like it was coming
from behind a door. My ears were still messd up
from the gunshots. She told me to rite my full name.
I put down Bunny O'Toole and ast if that was OK.
My names Bernard but no 1 ever calld me that xept
Grampa. She said Bunny was OK.

Im Sarjent Nolan but you can call me Nikki she said. Like Nikki K the rapper—you no her dont you?

O yah I said but I dint reely.

The paper was yello with lines. The pen was the kind that went *blob blob* wen you rote. Now your address said Nikki so I put that down—2 Tecumsee. I ast did she want Trono and Canada and that. She shook her head.

And how old r you Bunny? Rite that too.

I put down 15.

You sure you dont want sum thing to eat? You look hungry.

Well mayb a muffin.

OK.

She told me to rite down what happend in my own words. I ast what she ment by my own words and she said what do you member?

Starting ware? I said.

At the start.

Like wen we got to Sure Way and the Angels and Buffalos were there with there bikes and the SUV and then the pleece cars came?

Befor that.

Like driving to the mall?

Befor that.

Lunch? That was at Snocones house. There was a baby.

Befor that.

Befor lunch—like brekfast? I had that at home I said. OJ and Rice Krisps. Spencer likes them and Mom always makes sure there there.

By now Nikki was frowning the way evry 1 does at me. Not meen but tired you no? Like she wantd to say Jeez Bunny smarten up. Guys do that even if they all reddy no Im a dummy. Not Spencer but evry 1 els. Mom and Dad do. Mom sure does. I can see it in her face. She loves me but she wants to yell at me 2.

Sorry I said. I dont no what you want.

I wishd Spencer was there to xplane for me. But Spencer was off with Dad kissing that actress and getting lost and driving Mom crazy. I was here at the pleece stashun with Nikki the cop and she was giving me the Jeez Bunny look and rolling up her blu sleevs. A sister Jaden wud call her but I cant cuz Im not reely a brother.

Start at the begining she said. Wen did you join the possy?

The table was chippd and wiggly. There were marks on it like sum thing xploding. Other guys marks.

I told Nikki that I dint no I was in the possy until Jaden said so. That was wen he saw Grampas tatoo.

Your grampa has a tatoo?

No I do. Grampas dead. I got his tatoo for him.

I touchd my arm saying this. It still hurt a littl bit. I shud of bin rubbing that goop on it. Nikki ast cud she see the tatoo so I pulld up the sleev of my new shirt and there it was. Pretty sweet.

Why dont you start with that? she said. Wen did you think about getting the tatoo? Rite down evrything that happend from then until now OK Bunny? Ill bring you a muffin.

Evrything? I said. Thats alot.

Im no good at riting. I get words rong and I forget ware I am and my spelling is Very Bad. Thats what Miss Wing says. She helps me in skool. Shes hot. Evry 1 says so.

What if I dont do it? I ast.

Then youll go to jale said Nikki the pleece woman.

Was she kidding? She dint look like she was kidding. And I was in a pleece stashun. And bad

4

things had happend. Shots and things. I dint want to rite all the stuff down. But I dint want to go to jale.

Your meen I said. Your a meen lady you no that?

Yah. You want a coke with that muffin?

I side a long one. Huhhhhh.

I never herd of Nikki K I said.

She left and I bent over and startd riting.

WHEN IT BEGAN

WE WERE ON THE STREETCAR—all of us.
This was a wile ago like last week or the 1 befor.
Me and Spencer Mom and Dad scraping along
Queen Street past traffic lites and turning cars.
Past the take out place and the *SHOOS SHOOS
SHOOS* place and the place ware Spencer gets his
movys. Past the corner with the hobos and the corner
with the bank and the corner with all the shmata
stores—thats what Dad calls them anyway.
He xplaned but I forgot. Past the drug store and the
junk store and the restront and the other restront
and the other 1. Spencer was beside me watching

6

Kill Bill on his phone. Mom and Dad in the seat in front of us. The car was full. Peepl and smells and noys and more peepl.

Mom was quiet and Dad was patting her hand. She was waring good close. Me and Spencer too—shirts with buttons. Dad lookd funny without the bandana he normly has on.

I saw a topless girl on the sidewalk and poked Spencer. Then we were past her and she turnd out to be a guy not a girl. A fat guy jiggling. Ew.

What? said Spencer taking out his ear thing.

Nothing.

He went back to *Kill Bill.*

Sum thing Jewish. What shmata meens. Jewish for sum thing.

✼

Downtown the bildings were bigger and evry 1 had phones in there hands. We went round the door—I meen the door went round and we were in it. You no. And then we were in a big stone room with a seeling that went up and up. Very cool. I went Wow! and I cud here my voys going *wow ow ow ow* getting softer.

Hey I said.

Ey ey ey.

I did it agane. *Ey ey ey.* An old guy glared up at me.

Mom said Shhh!

Shh shh shh.

Made me laff.

In the elvater Mom was shaking her head at Dads cowboy boots and he was humming sum old song—he does that alot. My neck hurt from my shirt. Spencer was back to his movy. The elvater went up.

I was thinking about Grampa. He was reel old. Like the pine ears—that kind of old. He livd in a cottage by a lake. Leest thats ware we saw him. He livd other places 2 but I never saw him there. He was always old. His hair was white and his hands had those bumpy blu lines. He calld me Bernard. I kept telling him it was Bunny but he dint lissen. How r you getting on in skool Bernard? he said. R you playing sports Bernard? Your a big boy—sports r good for you.

He said that a lot about sports.

I said my name was Bunny.

You shud be on a teem. You learn a lot being on a teem. Your fast Bernard.

No Im not I said.

I meen your quik—your hands move fast. What r you good at?

Finding things I said. Mom says Im the best. She always gets me to help her find her keys.

I ment like baseball he said.

＊

I member telling him 1 time that I was sorry. He ast why and I said cuz I wasnt smarter. He told me not to be sorry. He ment this I cud tell. It was important to him. There was just the 2 of us standing on the dock cuz evry 1 els was playing tag or sum thing. He put his hands on my sholders and stared at me.

Never feel sorry for yourself he said. Never never never. Do you understand Bernard?

Im not sorry for me I said. Im sorry for you.

He took a step back and opend his mouth and then closd it agane. And then DJ came running up behind me and pushd me. Hes always pushing peepl. I cot his hand and we spun each other round like Grampa tot us that time in the barn. We pushd and pulld for a bit and then Grampa pushd us both into the lake—and that was pretty funny.

It dint look like him in the coffin. I hardly new him. I ast Spencer if it was reely Grampa or if it was like a doll or sum thing. Spencer said that was him all rite—he just lookd weerd cuz he was pumpd up with stuff.

Just befor the elvater got to our floor and went *ding* I jumpd in the air so I cud feel my lunch left behind—thats always fun. Mom gave me the Jeez Bunny look. The door opend and we went to the loyers offis. The room was full of uncles and antys and cuzzens—peepl I hardly ever see xept at the cottage. It was like a suprise party xept no 1 shoutd suprise. They were all stiff like they were made of cardbord. Mom went over and starting hugging Anty Vicky. Dad gave a peace sine to evry 1 and Spencer side. He says Jer is lame. That's what he calls Dad—Jer. Short for Jerry. I ast Dad if he wantd me to call him Jer too and he said it was a free country and I was a free sole and it was up to me.

Mom said I better not call her Deb. Its a free country but Im your mom she said.

We all sat down and the loyer talkd about Grampa for a bit and it was kind of boring—and then he talkd about a mistery part of Grampas will that had to do with us grand kids. He said sum of us wud have to leev the room and Steve and DJ startd shouting at each other—there brothers and they bug each other alot. But it all got sortd out and it was the parents who left. I was a bit worryd but I was beside Spencer and he told me we were cool.

My chair had a smooth seat and wen I movd it sounded like a fart. I laffd and felt better.

The loyer sat at the big desk and leend forward. He calld us jentl men—funny cuz we wernt. We talkd about what a suprising will Grampa had made and what a suprising guy he was. I thot about the time he hid in the walk-in freezer and scared the crap out of all of us 1 at a time. That was suprising all rite.

And then the weerdest thing of all happend. The loyer turnd on a TV set and there was Grampa himself on TV. He was sitting down in a chair and looking out at us saying good afternoon boys. I must of said sum thing cuz a cupl of them turnd to stare at me for a second. Spencer told me that it was all OK.

TV Grampa made a long speech about how grate we all were and how much we all ment to him. It was nice to here this stuff about us but it was weerd too. Grampa was saying these things but he was dead. And he cudnt count. He said there were 7 of us but there were only 6. I checkd—6. And agane making sure I countd myself. Still 6. I new these guys. All my life I new them. I ast Spencer what was going on and he told me to wate and see.

Grampa was talking about nvelopes now. Nvelopes for each of us and things he wantd us to do inside the nvelopes. I had no idea what he ment—what kind of thing cud I do for a dead guy? I meen reely. I stared at the TV but I cudnt get what Grampa was saying. He liftd his glass. His littl hat was off to 1 side and his wispy hair was sticking out from under it. And then the screen went black and that was that. Grampa turnd into nothing. Well I gess we all do eh? Lifes your TV show and then sum 1 switches you off.

I countd agane to make sure. 6 of us.

The room was buzzing—evry 1 talking and waving there arms. I herd sum of what they were saying but it dint make sens. Tasks we were sposed to do. Tasks for Grampa. I dint no what they ment. Tasks. Spencer was talking to Webb so I cudnt ast him. Sum 1 said how xiting it all was. Yah I no— xiting eh! I said. But I dint meen it. Then the loyer gave us our nvelopes—big brown 1s with our names on them. And our moms and dads came back in and there was more talk and arm waving. Mom was crying and so was Anty Vicky and Uncle John. I was thirsty but I dint see a fountin anyware so I gulpd inside my mouth and wated for sum 1 to tell me what to do next.

My nvelope said *BERNARD*.

✣

Our kitchen is yello. I like sitting at the table and watching the sun make dime end shapes on the floor. Mom was sniffling by the sink. Dad was rolling out a pi crust—he does that wen hes upset. It helps him think. Me and Spencer were at the table with our nvelopes in front of us.

I new what was going on now—Spencer xplaned on the way home. Grampa did a lot of things in his life but there were sum things he never got round to cuz he was working and stuff. Now Grampa was dead and we were going to do the things he never did for him. Thats what a task is—a thing you have to do. Me and Spencer and Webb and Adam and all the other grandsons were going to do the tasks Grampa dint do for himself. The nvelopes had jobs in them— 1 for each of us. I wantd to open my nvelope on the streetcar but Mom told me to wate. I ast what good it was to do a job for sum 1 who was dead. No 1 anserd. So now Spencer and me sat at the kitchen table with our nvelopes in front of us. And I had a drink of milk 2. And Mom gave a sniff and Dad put the pi crust into a pan and the oven buzzd to say how hot it was. And Spencer and I startd in ripping.

YOU WONT BELEEV

WHAT GRAMPA WANTD me to do. What my task was. Reddy? OK here it is. He wantd me to get a tatoo. I no isnt that crazy? Isnt that the weerdest thing? A tatoo. Wen I red the letter I went NO WAY and startd laffing. Spencer was all reddy dun with his letter and going O crap O crap O crap.

Grampa had it all plannd out for me. There was a tatoo place on Lake Shore run by an old bud of his and I was going to show up and the guy wud give me a tatoo. Grampa xplaned in his letter. He was sposed to get a tatoo back in 1945 with his crew—Grampa flew airplanes—but he was sick that day and they got the tatoo and he dint. And then the war ended and he came home and got bisy with other things so now he wantd me to get the tatoo for him.

I no your big and strong Bernard

he rote in the letter

so you can stand the pane of the needl. The tatoo will remind you of sum important things. Your not a kid any more. Your getting older. Your growing up and I bet you feel alone sum times. But your not alone. Evry time you look at your arm youll no your apart of sum thing big. Me and my crew never let each other down. We wont let you down ether. Together we fly. Thats our motto. Make it yours Bernard. Trust yourself and trust your teem. Dont do this for me—do it for you.

Sum thing like that anyway. I dont member the xact words. There was more stuff about being there for each other and all. I showd the letter to Mom. She was upset but I wasnt. Not even at the Bernard. I was used to it.

A tatoo—not bad. Lots of kids at skool have them. Ed sits next to me and has 2 arrows on his arm. There cool.

Poor old Spencer was hanging his head and moning. Gess what? He had to kiss an old lady. That was Grampas task for him—find sum old lady actress and get her to kiss him. Spencers into movys and all and I gess thats what Grampa was thinking. I laffd and laffd. Glad Im not you I said. Id rather get a tatoo than a kiss from sum creepy old bag. He told me to shut up.

The phone rang. Mom said *Vicky!* and then startd talking 649 miles a minit. I herd her say *Africa!* like she says *Your kidding!* I dint care about Africa. I went to the TV room and sat in the blu chair and wonderd about things. I dint no what good it wud do Grampa for me to get his tatoo. Or for Spencer to kiss his old lady. Or whatever the others were doing. Grampa was dead. His letter said *do it for you* but I dint get that ether. What wud a tatoo do for me? I wonderd if Spencers letter said do it for yourself and what a kiss from an old lady wud do for him? I turnd on the TV and found cartoons. OK then.

❋

Mom came into my room to say good nite. It was dark but I cud see her face in the lite from the hall. Her eyes were all skinny and her mouth was down at the corners. She ast how I felt and I told her fine.

And do you still want to get the tatoo? she ast.

Uh huh.

You dont have to she said. Just cuz Grampa ast you to do sum thing you dont have to do it. He was my dad but I dint always do what he wantd. If he ast me to get a tatoo Id say no. Tatoos r ugly Bunny. Ugly and stupid.

She stoppd and the word hung in the air for a bit. Like a fart you no? *Stupid.* I new Mom was wishing she dint say it. Stupid was what I was.

I wonderd did Grampa think tatoos were stupid? Was that why he wantd me to get 1? I dint think so. This wasnt about stupid. It was sum thing els.

I want to go tomoro I said.

She side.

Wate a few days she said. Wate and see if you still feel this way. Good nite now. And she left me alone in the dark.

✤

12 Street.

13 Street.

14 Street.

It was a few days later—Friday afternoon. I dint change my mind. I was sitting on the streetcar going along Lake Shore. I was on my way to Kilroy Tatoo. The streets we past were numbers and that made it easy for me. Kilroy Tatoo was at Lake Shore and 20 Street. All I had to do was count.

17 Street.

18 Street.

Mom was at skool. Its her job. Shes a prof. Prof O'Toole. Spencer xplaned what shes a prof of but I dint reely get it. Sum thing about how we no things—how we no what we no. I dint here the word Spencer used. You meen like flossing? I said and he laffd.

Thats a good 1 Bun man. Yah Mom teeches flossing.

So anyway she was at skool being a prof and Spencer and Dad were on there way to Buffalo to find his old lady and I was on the streetcar counting to 20. I was alone. Mom ast if I wantd her to go with me but I said no. I dint want her calling evry 1 with a tatoo stupid. Besides this was my task and Grampa wud want me to do it alone. If DJ cud go to Africa on his own I cud find a tatoo place.

Xept I cudnt. I got off the streetcar at 20 Street and lookd around but there was no Kilroy. I saw a junk store and a restront with a sine that blinkd *BUD BUD BUD* and a dollar store and a place with weel chairs in the windo and a fite but no Kilroy.

It wasnt a reel fite. A fat bully kind of kid was pushing a skinny 1. The big kid had teeth and a shiny haircut and was pushing so hard the skinny 1 fell down and wen he got up the fat kid pushd him agane. Push and push. And he was saying a word.

I dint like it. Big aganest littl isnt fair. I dint like the word ether.

It was getting dark and there was wind. I shiverd in my short sleevs. The skinny kid fell down. The big 1 said the word agane. I went over and told him to stop it. Hes littlr than you I said.

The big 1 turnd. And who r you? he ast.

Bunny I said.

The other kid got up and brushd off his pants. He was crickety with long skinny legs and arms and kind of bug eyes. He dint run away. He wasnt scared.

The big kid tryd to push me. I cot his hand in mine and held on and wen he tryd to pull his hand away I dint let him.

No I said.

His leg went back and he tryd to kick me. I saw his foot come at me and dint think what to do I just did it. I grabbd his foot and liftd the way I used to do wen Spencer and me were fiting. I still had the big kids hand so I liftd him off the ground and spun him round hanging on to his arm and leg. He wasnt laffing like Spencer tho—he was kicking with his other leg. I tossd him away from me. He went like that in the air and landed on top of a trash can and stayd there.

The other kid said holy crap.

There was a tatoo place across the street. Not Kilroy a differnt 1. I wonderd if theyd no about Kilroy so I crossd and gess what? It was the rite place after all. Kilroy retired and now the place was calld Ink Tank. Thats what the guy at the desk said. Grate I said. I told him who I was and he said sure sure. He had my name and evrything.

Down the hall and on your left he said.

SHE HAD THE NEEDL

IN HER HAND like a pen and amed it at my arm.
Reddy? she said and there it was. Sharp and fast like
litening. I cud feel it going up my arm to my brane.

O I said.

Did that hurt?

I memberd Grampas letter. *I no you can take the
pane Bernard.*

Im OK I said.

Her name was Roxy. She was bald and short like a
dorf. She wore an undershirt and shorts to show her
tatoos. She had riting all over her sholders arms legs
and neck. There was even riting across her bald head.

I dint want to stare so I dint reed the riting. It lookd cool but kind of gros 2.

Wen I came into the room she was picking papers off the floor. She threw them on a table and yond. She held up the top peace of paper. It had a 15 on it.

This is you rite? she said.

Huh?

Your ink. Your tatoo. What you want on your arm.

I said I dint no.

R you 15? she ast.

Yah.

That was what Grampa said in the letter. *Your getting older now Bernard.*

My birthday was last month I said.

OK whatever. Your 15 said Roxy. She put the paper on my arm and wet it and took away the paper and there was the drawing on my arm. There was a 15 and a candl like for a cake. Ill put it down here so you can see it. Like this. See?

Cool! I said.

You like that? You want it in ink?

Yah ink me I said.

Roxy yond. What a day she said. 3 jobs alreddy and an other after yours and Im tired as deth. I dint get any sleep last nite.

She got her needl.

Stay still she said.

I dint think about the pane. I sat in the chair and thot about Roxy working. She followd the marks on my arm stopping to wipe away the blud. Wen she yond I cud see the back of her mouth. Ew. I thot about what kids wud say about my tatoo at skool. Wen I saw Eds arrow tatoo I went Wow. I dint have a best frend or any thing but mayb sum 1 wud say Wow wen they saw my 15. Spencer wud say sum thing. Way to go Bunster or sum thing. Spencers OK.

Stay still said Roxy.

I countd holes. There were 17 of them on my rite hand wall and 9 on my left hand wall. Holes like from a hammer. I countd them agane. 9 and 17.

Roxy stood back and yond sum more.

Your dun she said. What do you think?

She held up a meer and there was the tatoo.
It lookd rong—like a 21. But that was the meer. It was
a 15 all rite.

Wow I said.

There was a bit of blud. Roxy wiped it and put
on a big band ade. She used tape to hold it on.

Thanks I said and she smiled. She had a lip tatoo
and wen she smiled I cud see it. *LOVE*. Wen she
stoppd smiling the letters went away.

I hurt. Not litening bolts but it was there. Pane.
Roxy told me to by sum goop to rub on the tatoo
or els sum thing bad wud happen. She told me the
kind to get. Put it on 2 times a day for a week she said.
I said OK.

The guy outside in the hall was taking off his
button shirt. I dint see his face but he had a nife tatoo
on his rite sholder.

2 men sat in the wating room talking about me.
I cud tell cuz wen they saw me they stoppd. Older
men like 30 or 50. 1 of them had a vest and long
hair. You the 1? he said.

What 1? I said.

You hurt that Angel across the rode. Dint you?
The Angel hassling Jaden?

Uh I said.

Yah your the 1. I saw. But you not 15 r you? You 15?

He was frowning.

Yah Im 15 I said.

Huh! You dont look like it he said.

I get that all the time. Im big but I dont look very old.

But its cool he said. You keep on hurting those Angels. Who they think they r anyway?

Uh huh I said. I was playing with the band ade— pulling at the tape and lifting it up so I cud look at the tatoo. Then sticking it back down agane. I lookd up and he was staring at my arm. My tatoo. The other man was peeking 2. He had thick glasses.

This kid a brother? he said.

Shut up TJ said the long hair 1.

He dont look it is all.

Shut up TJ. Hes with the possy. You see the ink?

I dint no what they were talking about.

It was a yucky gray day but I felt like walking. I countd the blocks back words. 20. 19. 18. I peeld back my band ade and there it was. My tatoo. I cud feel it with my hart going. *Bump bump bump.* Arm arm arm.

I wantd Spencer to see my tatoo. I peeld away the band ade and held out my phone and twistd my arm round and took a pick sure. Not bad. You cud see the 15 and candl sort of. I sent the pick sure to him.

I thot *I did it.* All the cuzzens with all the tasks and I did mine befor any 1 els. Im the winner. I checkd my tatoo agane. Did I feel Grampa with me? No. The tatoo was mine not his. He wasnt 15. I was.

Arm arm arm.

I came to a drug store and that reminded me I had to get the goop to rub on my tatoo. A lady showd me the rite kind. She wantd to see the tatoo but wen I showd her she stoppd smiling.

Whats rong? I said.

She dint say any thing just backd away covering her mouth.

Weerd.

Poring rain wen I got outside. Poring like a flud. Peepl stood under the overhang watching the rain splosh and grrgle wating for it to slow down.

I checkd my phone. Nothing from Spencer. I sent him a text—did u look yet? tel me. Then I had to look agane myself so I pulld off the band ade.

Not bad.

A kid was watching.

Hey! he said to me. He new me and I new him. He was the skinny kid from outside the tatoo place. The 1 getting pushd round.

He stared at the tatoo then at me.

Now I no he said.

What? I said.

Why you hurt that Angel. Your 15 arnt you?

Evry 1 wantd to no how old I was. Yah I said. I put the band ade back down. It dint stick very well any more.

He held up a fist and changed it to a hand wide open. Like a bom xploding.

What? I said.

He did it agane. Fist—hand open.

I nodded and did the same thing back to him.

He nodded 2.

How old r you? I ast.

14 he said. But I bin in the possy forever. Cobras my brother so they let me in erly. I no the sines. Look here.

He pulld down a wet sock to show me a tatoo. Gess what it was.

Hey its like mine I said. Xept for the candl.

You dont look 15 he said. And I never seen you befor. But you got the ink and you no the sines.

I never seen you ether I said.

So ware you bin? How come I dont no you.

I live away from here I said.

Away? O yah—away. I get it he said. I no lots a guys who had to go away. How long were you away?

How long?

Your talking about jale rite? Cors you r. Thats why I dont no you. You bin away. How much time you do?

I dint no what he ment so I smiled and he smiled back. He came up to my chin or a littl past it. His hair was thick and curly. Im Jaden he said. What do they call you?

I told him.

O yah what you told the Angel he said. Thats funny. Thats cool. Bunny.

He put out his hand and I thot we were going to shake but he leend close and grabbd me near the elbow. So I did the same thing to him. My hand

29

went all the way around his arm like I was holding a hocky stick.

Your differnt he said.

I no.

Does it bug you? Being—

Dum? Im used to it.

I meen your white.

Well Im used to that 2 I said.

We were still holding on to each others arms. He was black—not black black but pretty black. You no what I meen.

Does Scratch give you a hard time about it? he said. Or Jello? I gess they leev you alone cuz of the candl.

He pointd at my tatoo.

I no what the candl meens he said. I respect you Bunny. You did what you had to for 15. Like you did with that Angel today. You threw him away like trash. That was aw sum. Man that was proper. Sum seeryus you no?

He let go of my arm then.

I respect you 2 I said.

I dint no what he was talking about with his jale and candl. I dint no Scratch and Jello were guys names then. But I new Jadens smile was reel and it was for me.

Im going to the jim on 15th he said. You want to come and hang out?

With you?

Yah. Im part of the possy he said. Dont be shamed of me. Cobra trusts me. I no stuff he said.

Im not shamed I said. I like you.

Thing was I wasnt used to going around with any 1. I was used to being alone.

Itd be cool to hang out at the jim I said. But I cant rite now. I need to check in with my mom.

He nodded a cupl times.

Mom. Rite. Your talking about your prole offiser rite? I forgot you just got out of jale. My brother used to call his PO Mom too.

Mayb Ill come to the jim later I said.

His face britend—it reely did.

Ill look for you he said. Morgan runs the place. You no him rite?

Uh I said.

Well anyway its on 15 Street beside the king pizza place.

OK I said.

A streetcar was slowing down in front of the drug store. Water splashing off the tracks. Doors opend and peepl hurryd off and on.

Well—by I said. By Jaden.

By Bunny.

I ran thru the rain.

AT DINNER

IT WAS JUST ME AND MOM. I showd her my tatoo wen I got home and she said O deer and lookd away fast. I put back the band ade. She kept looking at my arm and then looking away. I new she hated the tatoo so I put on a long shirt for dinner. The blud was gone but it still hurt even with the stuff on it. Arm arm.

We ate in front of the TV sins it was just the 2 of us. It was Dads stew from last nite. I had 4 carrots and 2 chickn chunks and 4 potatos. Mom hates cartoons and sports so we watchd an old guy talk to an other old guy across a table. I ate the carrots and potatos first and countd my chews. 20 and a swallow. I do that sum times. 20 more and an other swallow.

I told Mom about Jaden. Were frends even tho were differnt I said.

She said that was grate. Evry 1 is differnt she said. Now shhh.

The old guys on TV were fiting about sum thing. Your rong said 1. No your rong said the other. They both had gray hair and shirts and tys and glasses. They were the same. They even shook there heads at the same time.

Last bite. 17 18 19 20. Swallow. I was dun. I ast if I cud go out. Mom dint anser. I ast agane. Its Friday and theres no skool I said.

Mom turnd. You want to go out? Ware?

My frends jim. He ast me. I no ware it is. Its 1 streetcar. Pleas mom.

You have your phone rite? And you no the rules—home by 9.

Yes.

OK then.

She turnd back to the TV.

Grate! Thanks Mom. Im on my way.

Mom said shhh.

✥

The streetcar stoppd rite at 15 Street. I walkd past places that fixd cars and places that sold candy and places that I dont no what they did and places that dint do any thing cuz of the bords in the windo. I saw guys smoking and moms pushing babys. Evrything smelld good after the rain. Even the smoke. Peepl stared at me out of the side of there eyes.

The jim was easy to find—big brick bilding with no windos. No door ether and I was staring at it and wondering how to get in wen I herd my name. Jaden came out of the pizza place next door with 2 slices in his hand.

I was wating for you he said witch made me feel good. He took me round the back. The wall beside the door had my tatoo on it. 15 with stripes. Weerd eh—a wall with my tatoo.

What was Grampa thinking?

We went into a hall with a bare lite bulb and a smell that was not as nice as the after the rain smell.

Pretty bad reely. Down the hall was a wide open room with brite lites. There was a boxing ring and wates and a punching bag off to the side. And a guy who came over and said Who the hell is this?

Jaden said Hi Morgan this is Bunny. Bunny this is Morgan.

He gave Morgan 1 of the pizza slices. I said hi.

Morgan was a grone up—had a beerd and all. His nose was flat and his eyes were sort of skinky at the corners. He had a wistle round his neck like a ref.

What you doing here boy? he said to me.

I dint no what to say.

Show him Bunny said Jaden.

Show him?

Your ink. Your tatoo.

OK I said. The band ade came up with my sleev and there was the 15. Morgans eyes opend wide.

Ware you get that? he ast me.

Bunnys bin in hall said Jaden. Thats ware he got the candl. Thats why you dont no him. Hes OK.

Morgan still lookd—I dunno.

What hall you in? he ast. That juvy place out in Scarboro? Bonesaw was there and I herd it was pretty bad. You there boy? Or sum ware els?

So many questions and I cudnt anser any of them. I countd black drips. 1 2 on the floor then a bunch on the wall 3 4 5 6 7.

Jaden was talking.

Bunny saved my ass today he said. Shud of seen him throw this big Angel away. Bunny nose the sines. Hes with the possy Morgan.

2 guys were in the ring going round and round. They were dressd like UFC fiters—tite shorts and littl gloves and that was all. The fiter in black shorts was good. He was kind of fat but he movd fast.

That inks fresh—ware you get it dun? Morgan ast.

I new this anser. I told him about the Ink Tank place and Roxy the dorf and he ate his pizza and nodded.

I saw old Billy from Ink Tank this afternoon. Told me sum thing about a white boy hurting an Angel on the street. That you? Billy said you threw the Angel round like he was a frisbee or sum thing.

What I told you Morgan said Jaden. Bunny here was saving me.

Xept I dint no that guy was an Angel I said.

The fiter in black nockd the other 1 down with a hammer to the neck. Morgan blew his wistle and told them both to stop. Then he went back to looking at me.

So Bunny—how you get to be 15?

I dint no what he ment. I was 14 last year and now Im 15.

It just happend to me I said. Same as any 1.

The fiters were leening on the ropes staring down at us. Black Shorts had a tatoo like Jadens and mine and the wall out side. This was weerdr and weerdr.

Your name reely Bunny? he said. Like a bunny rabbit?

I said yah and ast what his name was. He jumpd down from the ring and walkd over. His belly hung over his shorts.

His names Jello. Cuz he got a jelly belly.

Shut up Jaden. You just a kid.

Jello movd easy. He was in shape. His hair was shavd so I cud see his skull underneeth. He had reel black skin—blacker than Jaden or Morgan.

There were flys all over. Jello swiped at 1 and it buzzd away.

So you tuff he said to me. You a tuff Bunny. A killer like Scratch. Can you fite? Mayb you can toss sum Angel on the street. Mayb you put down sum guy in hall—white guy I bet. But can you take on a brother?

A brother? I said.

He dint meen Spencer. I can nock Spencer down evry time. We dont fite any more. We never did much but its bin a long time now.

I dont want to hurt any brother I said.

Dint think so. You not 15. I wont beleev it til Cobra says so.

His words hung in the air in front of me. Like a sheet or sum thing. A curtin.

Cobras coming said Jaden. You wate Jello. Wate and see. Hey Bunny you want sum thing to drink?

Mayb I shud go I said.

Yah said Jello.

No—wate for Cobra.

There was 2 flys buzzing around my head. I grabbd them both. I dont like flys.

Huh! said Morgan. You got fast hands Bunny.

Jaden and I drank coke wile Jello went over to the punching bag and startd in punching. He was good. The bag was jumping round. Morgan was with him but kept looking back at me. Jello wud punch the bag and Morgan wud look at me. The other fiter came over to ware we were on the couch and hung his head. I cud see his ribs go in and out wen he took a breth. Jaden calld him Xray.

Wo he said.

Wen I was dun my coke I went over and pickd up a wate. It said 20 on it so I thot I wud lift it 20 times. Wen I got to 20 I put it down and my phone rang.

IT WAS SPENCER.
HEY! I SAID.

HE SAID HEY BACK and we talkd for a wile.
He told me he got my shot of the tatoo and it was
cool. His words went in and out. I pushd the phone
into my ear so I cud here him. He ast sum thing about
the 15. I told him about Jaden and the possy. Im in
I said. I ast him if he got his kiss. Not yet he said.
They were in a place calld Torrents. I ast if Torrents
was in Buffalo cuz I thot thats ware Spencer was
going. No he said it was Torrents Ontario and he
was there with an other guy insted of Dad. And get
this—Spencer was driving. He told me all about it.

Al Capoli? I said. Your with Al Capoli? And your driving a white convert able car?

Not bad I thot.

I herd a gasp and turnd round. A stranger was staring at me. He must of come into the jim wile I was on the phone. He was like 7 feet tall. I came up to his shirt. He was thin but not week. Bendy like a bow like he was reddy to shoot arrows at you. Cool guy with a super cool tatoo on his neck—a snake with fangs.

Al Capoli? he said to me.

He must of herd me.

I coverd the phone. Im talking to my brother I said.

Al Capoli from Buffalo? he said.

Yah.

Jaden stood next to the tall guy. Cobra this is Bunny he said. Pointing at me. You no him rite?

Evry 1 was staring at me—Morgan and Jello and Xray and Jaden and Cobra.

I wavd hi to Cobra.

Is Al Capoli in Torrents now? he ast. I nodded my head. You no how your talking on the phone and talking to sum 1 in the room at the same time? Thats how I was talking to Spencer and to Jadens brother.

42

Al Capoli is in Torrents Ontario in a white convert
able I said to Cobra and he threw his hands in the air
and walkd away.

I went back to Spencer. He was glad things were
cool with me. I told him I was pumpd and he said
that was xellent but that he had to run. I made a joke
and said wasnt he driving? Insted of running you no.
He said yah and later and hung up.

✤

9 oclock soon. I shud be going.

Cobra was holding a sell phone. I wud like to
talk to Rocko or Al he was saying. This is Cobra from
15 Street. I have got sum thing for you. Give me a call.

Your brothers tall eh? I said to Jaden. He dint anser.

The wate on the floor next to me was pretty big.
It had a 35 on it. I dint feel like lifting it 35 times.

Cobra came over to me. Bent down.

How do you no so much? he ast.

His head was close to my head. Was he joking?
No 1 ever thinks I no so much.

Capoli is missing he said. Rocko Wings does
not no ware he is. No 1 in Buffalo nose ware he is.

But you do. Strange white kid out of no ware. How is that? he ast.

I dint say any thing. Cobra was 2 big. Not just tall but—there—you no? He took up room. I cudnt think next to him.

Your a mistery Bunny he said. A reel mistery. Who did you kill?

What?

He pointd at my arm.

That says your in the possy he said. Says your a killer. Jaden told me you were inside. I have bin inside 2 and I no there r bad guys in there. Sum times you can work with them and sum times you cannot. Sum times you have to step up. Rite Bunny? Step up for yourself and for your frends.

Things were weerd here. Evry 1 was black and tuff and staring at me and I dint no why xept that I wasnt black. Cobras eyes were like lazers flashing inside me. I dint no what he ment about being a killer. I feel stupid looking back but I reely dint. Grampa wud call us killer sum times and he was kidding. Hey killer he wud say to DJ or Webb or Steve. Hey killer hows it going? I dint no what was going on here so I nodded at Cobra. Jaden stood next 2 his brother smiling at me. I did no about Jaden—leest I thot I did.

Step up for your frends I said. Yah.

I was thinking about Jaden.

Cobra undid buttons on his shirt and pulld it aside. There was a 15 with 3 candls.

Do you see that Bunny? he said and I said yah. You no what it meens rite? It meens I am not scared to step up for the possy he said. And nether r you. The possy comes first. Rite?

Rite I said. Frends first.

Say it. Say your 15.

He was doing up the buttons agane.

Sure I said. Im 15.

Sum thing was rong about the tatoo. Why was my 15 all over the place? I dint no but I kept on saying yah like I always do. Cobra thot I was tuff and that made me happy. He held out a fist and I did 2 and we did our xploding together. He calld evry 1 over and put his hand on my sholder.

This here is Bunny he said.

Jaden smiled. Morgan nodded. Jello dint look happy. Xray was still shaking his head and saying wo.

Cobras phone rang and he jerkd it open rite away.

Hello Rocko he said. Did you get my message?

THE NEWS WAS ON

WHEN I GOT HOME. Mom was in her chair. I dont like the news so I was standing in the door getting reddy to go up stares wen the pleece cars and yello tape came on the screen and the news guy said sum thing about Angels.

What Angels r they talking about? I ast Mom.

A gang she said. Mimico Angels. There from west of here. See on the TV—thats the subway stashun.

Whats rong with these Angels? I ast.

They do awful things she said.

On TV 2 pleece men put a guy into a car. He had a black beerd and vest like a pirate. The car door closd and that was the end of the news and we went to a girl opening a can of cat food.

Nite Mom I said.

Nite.

I went online to see ware Spencer was. It took me a wile but I finally found Torrents. It dint look far from Trono but nothing looks far on a map does it? I meen China and Peru r only this far apart. You can cover Africa with your hand.

I put on my goop. There was no blud and the tatoo dint hurt much. I flexd my arm and the 15 movd. I went to bed and thot about that bully and Jaden. I thot about Cobra with his hand on my sholder and Jaden smiling.

❋

Mom went off to be Prof O'Toole and tell peepl more about how we no what we no. I was alone in the house. Sum times Im alone cuz Spencers watching a movy in his room and Dads riting in the basment—not reely alone. Today was differnt 2— I was reely alone. I had my tost and jam and TV and I had a place to go after. I was so xited I cud hardly eat my brekfast. Goop on the tatoo and out the door. Morgan was sweeping the jim wen I got there.

Well well he said. Look whos here.

He was the only 1 around. I ast ware Jaden was. He said he dint no but did I want to work out wile I was wating? Help yourself he said and went back to sweeping.

I was lifting the 20 wate wen Morgan came over and said I was doing it rong. He showd me. His arm was huge.

I tryd it his way but it was harder. I cant do 20 I said.

OK how about 12?

But it says 20.

12 is fine he said.

He ast if I wantd to try fiting and I went yah. I like fiting I said.

I dont fite at home cuz Mom and Dad hate it and Spencer cant. And no 1 pix on me at skool any more. But theres fiting on TV. Spencer and I watch UFC sum times befor Dad changes the channel. I try to see how the guys do the moves.

Your fast said Morgan. I saw you catch those flys yesterday. You have fast hands.

I gess I said.

We climed into the ring.

First thing is to lern how to fall he said. Your going to get hit and you have to no how to fall safe and fast. Lets do it here in the ring cuz its a soft floor.

I can fall I said.

Yah? Show me.

And he nockd me down. His hands came out of noware and hit me in the chest and his leg was behind my foot and I fell to the floor and lay there going O. I wasnt hurt—just suprised. I climed back onto my feet.

Pretty slow said Morgan. With a littl smile on his face.

No fair I wasnt reddy I said.

Fiting isnt about being fair Bunny. Your a kid and I used to be a pro. That isnt fair ether. Trust me— you want to lern how to fall.

I was staring at him.

For reel? I said. A pro fiter like on TV?

Yah.

Like UFC?

Yah. Now watch me.

He went down but befor I new how he was back on his feet.

And thats with my bad leg he said.

I ast if he new any of the UFC guys on TV now. He said no. It was a wile ago he said. He was traning in a New York jim and they were all going to sine sum TV deel only he broke his leg in a practis fite and never came back.

And it happend cuz I dint fall rite he said. I got my leg twistd and sum 1 jumpd on me and it snappd.

Ew I said.

You try now he said. Try falling.

I did. Try agane he said. So I did it agane. Tuck in your sholder he said. Dont land flat. Land rolling. Hit like a brick and fall like a ball.

What?

Its what they say.

I smiled. Nice I said.

I fell agane. And agane. And agane. My sholder was hurting but I was getting the roll and Morgan said I was doing better.

Jello came in and ast what I was doing there.

Looks like you want to fite he said. He had on sunglasses and a stripy shirt and was eating a donut. You want to fite white boy? Do you? Ill fite you. Ill beet you like a drum he said.

I dunno said Morgan. Bunnys pretty fast.

Like a drum said Jello.

But just then Jaden came running in and ast did I want to do sum thing for Cobra? Sure I said. So I left without fiting Jello. I told him mayb later and he said any time at all. He tryd to push me but I got out of the way.

I thot about what they said. Hit like a brick and fall like a ball. Cool eh?

THE SUN WAS
BEHIND US

WALKING UP THE STREET. My shadow was bigger than Jadens—his was like a bunch of sticks walking beside my big lump. He was talking about tagging. Thats what we were going to do. We were going to do sum tagging today.

Like the game? I said.

What game?

Tag.

He laffd. Your funny he said.

I ast did he no about Morgan being a pro fiter? Jaden dint like fiting at all and dint want to talk about it. OK I said. We walkd sum more and then he stoppd so I did 2.

Wud you look at that? he said.

What?

He was pointing at a brick wall—the front of a place with bords on the windos. Uh huh I said but dint no what I was looking at.

Those dam Angels he said. Tagging on our turf. This is—15 Street. They cant put there tags here.

Huh? I said.

Well look!

Lots of riting and drawing on the brick wall. Differnt things. In the middl of the wall was a big white letter *A* with a littl *O* on top. Like this:

Thats there tag? I said.

Jaden was carrying a nap sack. He pulld out a spray can and sprayd out the sine in red. Then he took a can of black and sprayd a 15 on top of the red.

Wont they be mad? I ast.

Who?

Whoever lives here. Were riting on there house.

No 1 lives here stupid he said with a smile and a push.

The smile was reel and that made it OK. 1st time ever sum 1 calld me stupid and dint make me feel bad.

15 like my tatoo I said.

Were the 15 Street Possy arnt we? Thats our tag. Any 1 sees that sine they no that 15s bin here.

O yah I said. Cors.

So now I new about tags. It was a way of saying we r here. We. R. Here.

Me and Jaden went up and down 14 and 15 and 16 Streets looking for Angel tags and spraying over them. They were on bildings and streetcar stops and sidewalks. There was a big *A* on the side of a donut shop. I went inside and ast if it was OK to spray over it. The guy behind the counter dint no what I was talking about and Jaden draggd me out of there and said I was crazy.

That guy dont care about whats on his store he said.

O I said.

My fav was 1 we did on a STOP sine. The Angels had put *A* under the *O* to make it look like there tag. Jaden made a new tag for us on the sine. He sprayd out the *A* and then—you no how *S* looks like 5? Jaden put a white *1* in front of the STOP and fixd the *S* to be more like a 5 so the sine lookd like 15 TOP—like were the top. Cool or what? He climed onto my sholders to get hi enuff.

This was his job—looking for other tags. Its why the Angel bully was pushing him down wen I met him—he dint like Jaden spraying out his tags.

I look after the possy on the street he said. We have to be able to say this is our turf.

Turf I said.

Ware we r. Ware we hang out. Other gangs come along and tag on our turf and I rub them out.

Like picking up dog poop I said. You dont want those Angels pooping on our front lon.

He laffd agane. Your a funny Bunny he said.

It was lunch time so we went back to the donut shop with our tag on it. I got cool running shoos for my birthday and also money and I had sum money left so I bot us donuts and coffee. I wud of got coke but Jaden said coffee so I did 2 even tho I never had it befor.

I put in milk and 4 sugars like he did. We took our lunch down to the lake. Theres stones and garbaj and stuff and we went rite down to the water and climed big flat stones and stood there drinking and eating. The lakes so big you cant see across. The world looks flat all the way. The coffee was pretty good.

A bird landed near me and startd yelling. It went rite up to me and opend its mouth and yelld. Gimme it said. Gimme gimme gimme gimme. I still had sum donut left and I was going to give the bird sum and then an other 1 landed and started the same thing. Gimme. And an other 1 and an other. White birds with yello beaks and meen eyes. They were all round us going Gimme. I cudnt give them all donut so I ate it.

I ast if the Angels had turf. Jaden said of cors they did. Over by Mimico Street. I said we shud put our tags there and his face lit up. Thatd be aw sum he said but weed have to ast Cobra first. So we did— we went back to the jim and ast Cobra and he said no. He dint want any 1 messing with the Angels.

Not now he said.

That Angel guy was messing with me yesterday said Jaden.

That was away over on 20th said Cobra. And you were bugging the guy wernt you? Following him and spraying over his tag as soon as he put it on?

Mayb said Jaden.

We were all in the offis—a littl room off the jim smelling like smoke and swet. Cobra and Jello were sitting on the couch and watching TV. Cobras head was on a level with ours—Jadens and mine.

I dont want any problem with the Angels until after the deel goes thru he said.

O yah the deel said Jaden.

They both turnd to look at me.

You dont no any thing more about that do you mistery boy? said Cobra.

What? I said.

The deel said Cobra.

What deel?

The 1 with the Angels and the guys from Buffalo. You new ware Al Capoli was. Hes part of the deel—Rocko says so. Do you no sum thing you havent told us?

My brothers the 1 in Torrents I said. He textd me agane but it wasnt about the deel.

You sure? said Jello. What was it about? Lets see.

He stood up and came over to ware I was standing.

What did your brother tell you? he ast. You guys talking about our deel on the phone? Show us.

Yes show us said Cobra. The tatoo on his neck was dark ink xept for the eyes and fangs witch were red. Pretty intens.

I got out my phone. See? I said. Heres my text saying my tatoo still hurts. And heres what Spencer sent back.

I held my phone flat and we all stared at the screen together—me and Jaden and Cobra and Jello. The text said—outhouse xploded tell u later.

What the hell does that meen? ast Cobra.

I had no idea.

MOM WAS IN A GOOD MOOD

WEN I GOT UP THE NEXT DAY. She was in the kitchen with her coffee and her golfing hat and those shorts that make her look like 2 peepl. She said hi and did I sleep all rite. I said uh huh. And how about you?

Fine.

The coffee smell reminded me of the donut shop. I pored sum into the mug and put in lots of milk and sugar. The sun was shining and the floor of the kitchen was yello dime ends.

Mom had her phone out. Isnt that grate she said. What?

I got a text from your father. He says he and Spencer r having so much fun on there trip. He sounds reely xited.

Did he say any thing about the outhouse blowing up? I ast.

What r you talking about Bunny? Outhouse? What outhouse? There in New York City. There r no outhouses in New York City Bunny.

O I said.

I have to think about restronts for them she said. Your father and I went to a wonderful place down in so ho. I wonder if Spencer wud like it.

Im used to being rong. In histry class if I think the anser is the pine ears and sum 1 says the anser is water vaper then water vaper is probly rite and it probly isnt histry class. Thats what I am used to. But I was pretty sure I wasnt rong this time. Spencer said they were in Torrents. Not New York. I dint think he wud tell me a ly. But if there was a problem he mite ly to Mom. A problem like the outhouse xploding.

What is it Bunny?

I wasnt used to lying. But I dint want to give Spencer away.

Nothing I said.

She put away her phone and got her golf clubs out of the closet. She goes golfing evry Sunday with sum other profs. Dad laffs at her for being boor jaw. Its 1 of his things—he hates the boor jaws. She tells him to shut up but shes smiling wen she says it so its OK.

On her way out she gave me a hug.

Ill be back in the afternoon she said. You have my sell number.

OK.

Ware will you be?

I dunno. With Jaden I gess.

Good. Thats good.

She stood in the door looking back at me.

Have fun today she said.

You 2 I said. Get a bird.

Is that coffee? Wen did you start drinking coffee?

Yesterday I said.

And that was tru. I dint have to ly all the time.

The streetcar stoppd. Cars around us were honking. No 1 moving as far as I cud see. The driver said there was an axident and let us off. I startd walking. I went the same way the streetcar wud of bin going. After a wile I came to the axident. No blud or any thing just cars and pleece and toe trucks and glass. The Lake Shore was clear now but no streetcars. I kept walking.

I saw a hole lot of tags on fences and bildings as I walkd by. And on the side walk. Differnt sizes but all white and all the same kind.

Angel tags. I gess they were there all along but I saw them now cuz I was walking and cuz of what me and Jaden did yesterday. I past a sine that said *Mimico*. The rode bent round. A cupl of guys stood outside a corner store. They yond and smoked and spat. Wen I past they spat at me and told me to go away. I kept walking. It was a sunny day but I felt cold.

I herd a bike far away. That farting sound they make—*brrrap*.

The stores all had Mimico in the names. Mimico Hardware. Mimico Bar and Grill. Mimico Daycare. The bike sound got louder. It was going faster now and the sound was more like *vroom*. I went faster 2. I tryd counting my breths. In 2 3 4 out 2 3 4. I came to the number streets.

There was a junk store with a big Angel tag on the front. A guy with a beerd was going in. He stoppd and stared at me. I kept going. At the next lite the bikes cot up to me. 2 of them. The lite was red and the bikes were going *brrrap* and the guys were pointing at me. They both had jackets with the Angel sine on the back.

In 2 3 4.

I was all alone. The Angels were the bad guys. I felt it. I wantd to see sum 1 from 15—Jaden or Morgan or Cobra. Even Jello. I wud of bin happy to see Jello even tho he dint like me.

I textd Jaden hoping he wud text back and I wudnt be alone.

The bikes went slow like they were wating for me to catch up. I duckd down 3 Street so I cud miss them. At the first corner I turnd and startd running. In 2 3 out 2 3. I herd the bikes. They made a *vroom* sound now. They were coming after me. I took the next left. And the next rite. I dint stop to think about what the bikes wud do to me. Probly nothing.

Probly just laff. These were streets with houses and kids on wagons and guys cutting there front lons. I dint think about that. I dint think about us doing a deel with the Angels. All I new was that they were the bad guys and they were after me. In 2 out 2 in 2 out 2.

The Angels gave up and vroomd away the noys getting softer and softer. I took a big breth and kept going. Wen I got to 9 Street I saw my first 15 tag and felt warm inside. Weerd eh? Last week I dint no what a tag was. On 10 Street there was a big place with lots of peepl coming out and music 2. Today was Sunday. We dont go to church cuz Mom and Dad say theres no God but lots of peepl do go and this was a church. The music sounded nice and the peepl were dressd up and smiling at each other. And there was Jaden. He was with an old lady in a big white hat. Wen he saw me he ran rite over.

Bunny!

He was happy to see me—I new that. But he was sum thing els 2. He ast what I was doing there. I told him about the Angels chasing me and he shook his head and said yah. We made a plan to meet at the jim. He wantd to go home and put on new close.

You sure do I said.

He was waring a flower shirt and tite pants.

Shut up Bunny.

Just joking I said.

The church peepl dint like me. They dint smile or any thing. Most of them dint look at me. I ast Jaden who was the lady in the hat?

Who? O you meen Gramma.

He shut his mouth with a snap. He dint want to talk about her. See you soon he said and I said see you 2 and he walkd away down the street. Wen his gramma tryd to put her arm round him he shovd it off. He dint look back at me.

ALL AFTERNOON
WE TOOK TURNS

FITING IN THE RING. Morgan checkd our gear
and rang a bell and we went at each other. Me and
Xray and Jello and Snocone. I was pretty good. Fiting
is sum thing I can do. I cant run fast but my hands
can—I meen they go fast. They move on there own.
I dont try to make them do things but they do them
anyway. And Im sort of strong. I can lift stuff—like
desks and stuff. Dad calls me wen hes cleening the
kitchen and I get the frij out of his way.

The first fite was me and Xray who does marshal
arts with sum kind of belt. He kickd a lot and I kept
catching his feet. He dint like that. Wen I turnd away

he jumpd in the air to kick me from behind. I dint see him coming but my hand did. It movd on its own and pushd his leg in the air and he fell on his head and went uhhh. Yesterday he said wo—today it was uhhh. His hair spred out on the floor like a mop.

Poor Xray said Jaden.

Morgan climed into the ring to help Xray up.

I ast Jaden if he wantd to fite but he shook his head. He liked hanging out at the jim but he hated fiting.

And anyway I wudnt have a chance aganest you Bunny he said. Your good. You mite be as good as Jello he said. What do you think Morgan? He as good as Jello?

Probly not said Morgan.

He was holding Xray so he cud sit up. I ast Xray if he wantd to fite sum more. He tryd to say sum thing but all that came out was uhhh.

Morgan laffd.

Then Jello came into the jim. He had his fiting shorts on like befor and he pulld off his shirt and said it was his turn. He calld me white boy and ast if I was reddy.

Sure I said.

Morgan blew his wistle and Jello ran rite at me. I pushd him sideways to spin him and he was suprised and went down. I jumpd on him and got him in a key lock and his eyes got big and Morgan blew his wistle agane. The hole fite took like 10 seconds. Jaden cheerd. Jello told him to shut up and said I was lucky. He was panting and his eyes were small and mad.

1 more time he said putting his mouth gard back in.

Sure.

This time he went slower and I made a mistake and got 2 close. He swung left rite and wile I was catching his fists he need me rite there.

You no—there?

Wo that hurt.

He swung agane and I cudnt get my hands up in time and I went down and he fell on me. I wasnt breething yet. Morgan blew his wistle.

Got you said Jello.

Took me a wile to get back on my feet.

You dint drop and roll Morgan said to me.

I dint think you were sposed to kick there I said to Jello.

I fite 2 win he said. I do what I have 2.

We had a brake and Morgan took me a side. Who tot you to fite? he ast.

Tot? I said.

Your hands r so fast. I saw it yesterday and agane today. You missd Jellos rush and got him off balance. And then the lock. Sum 1 show you how to do that?

❉

Sum times at the cottage thered be fites. 6 boys and we all liked each other but we wud still fite. Weed be in the forest with no grone ups and DJ wud push sum 1. Adam or Webb wud start things 2 but mostly DJ. Hes bossy. 1 time we were all in the yard behind the barn and DJ pushd Steve down and then Adam pushd DJ down and we all got fiting and Grampa saw us and got the hose. We were wet and he was laffing and he took us into the barn and showd us how to do it better.

Dont push strate he said. Spin the other guy round. Thats how the empees did it back in the war.

Like this. And he hit Adams sholder and he spun round and down. Like this. And he hit Steves sholder.

Like this! said DJ and he tryd to hit my sholder but I cot his hand.

Good for you Bernard said Grampa.

After that we wud all try to do it—catch sum 1 on the sholder and spin him round. Spencer hated the game but I was good at it. Dad said it was OK at the cottage but I cudnt do it at home cuz it was too a gress of. I said I liked being a gress of. Dad said a gress of was bad.

❖

Want to lern sum more? Morgan ast me. Come here and Ill show you about kicking. We went over to the hevvy bag and he told me to side kick it. I did and he said No. Your close and 2 strate on he said. Start back and step into the kick. So I did that and it was better. Now turn your body wen your kicking said Morgan. You want to make the bag spin with your foot like you wud with your hand.

I thot about that and I kickd the bag like it was my cuzzen DJ and I was kicking his sholder. The bag movd a bit and Morgan nodded. There you go he said. Now do it agane. So I did. And agane and agane and agane. I tryd my left foot but I wasnt as good with that. Keep on said Morgan. Feet r stronger than arms. And longer. Now you no what to do if sum 1 comes at you with a nife.

What? I said.

Use your feet aganest a nife. You dont want to catch a nife in your hands he said.

A nife? I said.

He put pads on his hands and told me to punch them. He startd moving the pads around and I kept punching them. Good he said. Then he told me to kick and I did that 2. Morgan movd the pads faster and faster. Sum times he said kick and sum times he said punch. Jello came over to watch and I let my mind go blank and I kept hitting the pads. I dint miss ever. After a wile Morgan got tired and put down his hands and I took a big breth.

Good Bunny said Morgan. Reel good.

Good for a white kid said Jello. Hes good but not as good as me.

You hit harder than what he does said Morgan. You work on your wind and your ground and pound you going to go to the octagon 1 day Jello. But the kids faster.

I dont need you to tell me where Im going to go 1 day old man said Jello. I dont need you at all. And as for the kid Ill hurt him next time.

He turnd to me. I will he said.

We went to the room with the TV and sofa. There was a cooler with coke and beer. We were watching a nature show—bugs and things. Pretty gross. Jello came up behind me and said my name. I said hi and he punchd me in the face. Just boom without saying any thing. I cot his fist befor it landed.

Wide you do that? I ast.

He sat down next to me. He was shaking his head.

Man your *fast*! he said. No wonder they call you Bunny. How you get to be that fast?

I dunno I said.

We watchd the TV bugs for a bit. They were eating the hole forest.

You going to punch me agane? I ast.

I dunno he said and smiled so it was a joke.

I smiled back. And wonderd.

It was dinner time by my phone. I sent Mom a text that I wudnt be home for a wile. Im with my crew I said. Cuz thats what a possy is—a crew. And I was a reel part of it now. Xray sat next to me on the sofa with his head in his hands and wen I said I was sorry he said it wasnt my bad. His life suckd anyway—it just suckd more now.

Jello rolld his eyes at me. Xray talks like this all the time he said. Youll see.

Poor Xray said Jaden.

Wen Snocone nockd at the door of the jim I went to let him in and wen I gave the sine—fist and open—he gave it back to me. He had pizza boxes in the other hand.

Who r you? he said.

Cobra came up behind him. He had a long white shirt and a littl hat like a hocky puck on his head— like they have in Africa. Car keys in his hand.

Snocone this here is Bunny he said. Watch out for him. Hes a killer.

But hes—

White? Yah. He is. And who r you to talk?

Snocone had curly tite hair like a black guy but the hair was white. His skin 2—white like milk.

After the pizza we did sum more fiting. Jello beet Snocone and Xray and then I beet Snocone who was tricky fast but not very strong. Without sunglasses I saw his eyes were pink. Jello laffd at the 2 white guys in the ring. He wantd to fite me agane and I said OK. I tryd Morgans spin kick wen he ran at me but I missd and he pushd me down. He jumpd on me and tryed a kamora but I got my hand up in time to block. I wiggld my fingers on his ribs to try to grab sum thing and his mouth opend and he startd laffing and rolld off me.

No fair! he said. Morgan hes tickling me.

Morgan cudnt blow the wistle he was laffing 2 hard.

Secret wepon! yelld Jaden. Jellos ticklish!

I cudnt tell if Jello was mad or not. This isnt over! he said. The rest of us were laffing—but we stoppd wen the pleece broke in.

They said they nockd and we dint anser witch was why they broke down the door. They came into the jim with there guns out—2 3 6 8 of them. I countd. 8 cops spred out over the jim in there blu uniforms. They held up a paper and said they were serching the jim. Then they took us out thru the broke door and put us in pleece cars. Weerd eh? 1 of the pleece men took me aside.

What r you doing here? he ast witch was funny cuz I was wondering the same about them.

Your differnt he said.

DIFFERNT

IS WHAT MIKE CALLD ME back in Grade 4
wen I cudnt do up my shoos.

Evry 1 els in the class can do up there shoos
he said. And walk to skool. And tell time. You cant.

I walk to skool evry day I said.

With your brother.

I can do it by myself.

No you cant. Your differnt.

So we bet on it. He said Id get lost on my own
and I said o yah? and we made a bet. Next day I told
Spencer to go without me. I wated and then went out
the front door on my own. I wasnt worryd. I new my

way round. I walkd a lot. Spencer wud be watching a movy on his computer and Dad wud be doing londry and Mom wud be away and I wud walk. I new the streets and stores and parking spaces and hiding places by our house. I was good at finding things. I found the skool befor and I cud find it now. I walkd down our street to the silver house and across to the park with the broken slide and thru to the lane with the hobos sleeping. I said the root out loud as I went. Rite then strate then rite then left. Past the hobos and at the end of the lane I went left and there was the skool. Easy. I went rite up to Mike and said here I am. Here here here. Evry 1 round was laffing and pointing but I dint no why until Mr Ogden came over and ast ware my pants were.

I was so xited about the bet I forgot I had my pjs on. Witch is funny cuz they were yello with stripes and youd think Id notice.

My pants r at home I said.

Do you see any 1 els dressd like you? said Mr Ogden. Or r you the only 1?

He smiled round so evry 1 wud laff. He was that kind of teecher.

Im the only 1 I said.

I had to go home and change. The bet was for a pack of gummys but Mike never payd.

✦

I thot about this wen we were being lined up on the wall of the jim and 1 of the pleece men took me a side and ast me what I was doing.

Your differnt he said. You dont belong here.

And then a pleece woman pushd me back into line.

Dont be color blind Steve she said. Hes here. Hes part of the possy. He belongs. Dont you white boy?

She was taller than me. She put her hand under my chin and liftd my head up.

I said hi. She made a tuna face—like I make wen I get tuna for lunch witch Dad nose I dont like but he does it any way.

Your all the same she said and turnd away.

All the same I thot. All the same. Ha.

✦

Xray was with me in the back of the pleece car. What happens now? I ast him. Ware r we going?

Stashun. Ware you think?

The driver turnd on the siren and cut thru traffic. Xray put his head in his hands and startd moning. Poor old Xray.

This is so cool I said.

The pleece man in the front seat turnd round.

Your a happy 1 he said. You saying you want to go to the stashun?

Why not? I said.

We turnd uphill with the siren wooping the other cars out of the way. Stop sine. Stop sine. The sun was on my side of the car. Stop sine. We dint reely stop for any of these sines—slow down then fast agane. Xray moned evry time.

Hey r you the guy? ast the cop in the front seat. Phil is he the guy were sposd to watch for? Your name Jackson kid?

Whos Jackson? I said.

A frend of ours—guy the sarj said to look out for.

Shut up Tony said the driver.

I finally got a text back from Mom. ware r u?

I sent back in a pleece car.

I thot she wud be worryd but she wasnt. very funny.

I never no with Mom.

✦

They put me in a room by myself and closed the door. The lites buzzd and flickerd. Nothing happend. I slid down my chair and back up agane and sent Jaden a text. what now?

A fat pleece man came in with a tape recorder. He made me say my name and address into the tape recorder. His name was Sarjent Don. He filld up his chair. I dint. I kept sliding down and then trying to get back up agane.

Don ast me was I in the possy? I said I was. Then he ast about the deel we were planning. He new all about it.

You and the Mimico Angels rite? he said.

The Angels r the bad guys I said. They do tagging on our turf.

But you have a deel with them. Your working together. You and the Angels and the Buffalo mob.

O yah Buffalo I said.

We no a lot he said. But we need more if were going to stop the deel. Talk now and itll be better for you later. You dont want to go to jale do you? So help us. Talk. Will you talk to me?

Sure I said.

Wen is the deel going down? he ast.

I dont no.

Sunday? Monday?

I dont no.

Well what r you deeling?

I dint no what he ment so I dint say any thing.

Come on what? What kind of product?

I dint no why he was on me about this.

Ast Cobra I said. He nose. Or mayb Jello or Snocone I said. Dont ast Xray hes always moning. But Cobra wud no for sure.

Sarjent Don shook his head. His chins wiggld back and forth.

Tell us about the deel he said. Let us help you. You dont think so but were your frends Bunny. We r. You think Cobra cares about you? You think the possy cares about you? They dont. Sum thing goes rong they will throw you away. They will save themselves and you will go down. They dont care about you.

Yes they do I said.

So many things I dint no but I new this. Jaden cared about me. The others 2—mayb not as much

82

but they still cared sum. Cobra put his hand on my sholders and said this heres Bunny. I was part of the possy. They cared about me and I cared about them.

How did I no this? How was I so sure? I dunno. But I was.

They care I said.

Wens the deel? Don ast agane.

I dunno.

But there is a deel. You just said so. You said you dint no wen it was.

Im not very smart I said.

Get smart he said. Its smart to no who your frends r.

I was slipping down the chair agane. I pulld myself back up.

Don stoppd the tape recorder and got up to go. Befor he went he leend over and said he had to ast me sum thing. No tape he said. I just want to no.

What?

He leend forward and talkd soft.

I no how gangs work. What r you doing with 15 Street Bunny? Your the only face rite?

The only—?

I no wen Im in a room full of white peepl he said. I look around and I see theres no 1 like me and I feel differnt. Even if there my frends I feel differnt from them. Dont you feel differnt?

Don left and an other guy came in. He dint tell me his name. He had dark hair and littl eyes and his chin was blu. I stared at it. Blu. He ast the same questions as Don and wen I still dint no the ansers he got mad. Not the norml Jeez Bunny kind of mad. His mouth went all wide and he had bulgy things on his face.

Your LYING! he shoutd.

I dont—

I NO the kind of punk you r! You think you can SCARE me with THAT?

Pointing at my arm.

I am NOT scared. I am disGUSTd he said. That candl makes me want to PUKE! Your a SICK peace of CRAP kid. TALK to me or Ill HURT you! Ill put you in jale and you will NEVER get out. You cud go there NOW!

Im used to yelling but this was xtra loud and weerd. The guys face was dripping wet with swet.

He movd his mouth like he was chewing and then spit on the floor. He leend close.

TELL me! he shoutd.

What?

Ware the stash is. Wen the deel goes down. Its a 3 way deel—rite? Pipes for cash for hash? Who you talking to in Buffalo? WHO?

I shook my head. I had no idea what he ment. It was like he was talking french or sum thing. Or klingon or dog.

Your blu I said.

WHAT?

Like a smurf. You no? Your face is blu. Rite there.

I pointd. I saw now that his chin was stubbly. That was what made it blu. He slappd at my hand but I pulld it out of the way and he fell down. And just then the door opend and a pleece woman lookd in.

Loyers here Sarj she said.

Behind her was a guy in a soot and breef case. He pushd past her into the room and lookd at me and the angry pleece man who was back on his feet now.

Just what is going on here? said the loyer. R you questioning this boy? he said. You shudnt be.

Why r you hiding him? Ive bin all over this pleece stashun looking for him. R you trying to sum thing? R you? Do you no sum thing sum thing? This boys a miner. Look at him. You have no rites here. I will file a sum thing about you. Sum thing els 2. And sum thing sum thing sum thing els.

I dint understand a lot of what he said.

The angry sarj walkd out of the room with the loyer talking after him into the hall. Then the loyer came back in and kept going.

Did you say any thing to that cop? he ast me. Did you admit any thing? Did you sum thing sum thing? Did you sine any thing? If you did tell me now. Im your loyer. I can fix it.

I laffd.

Your like that guy on TV I said.

What?

The guy selling choppers. It does all these differnt things and never gets dull and its yours for 2 easy payments call now I said.

He talkd xactly the same as the chopper guy—so fast you dint here the words 1 by 1 but all in a bunch like a shower. His name was Julius and he was Jadens uncle but I dint find that out til the next day. He was the loyer for the possy. He got evry 1 els out of this place and now it was my turn.

A funny guy—he dint want to no any thing. Wen I startd to talk about what was going on he shook his head. Dont tell me he said over and over. If youve dun sum thing I dont want to no. Dont tell me any thing about plans or Angels or deels or guns or any thing. Now lets go.

Guns? I said.

I dont no any thing about guns he said. I dont no what your talking about.

Ware is Jaden? I ast. Wares evry 1?

I dont no he said. They were here and now there not. I dont no ware they r or what they plan on doing. And if you no—dont tell me!

We went down the hall reel fast. Pleece offisers were all over but we went thru them and out the front door of the pleece stashun. I dint no any of the bildings or streets. There was a statu on the side-walk—a littl kid pulling a wagon with a triangl thing on it. He lookd tired and I cud see why—the triangl thing was bigger than he was.

I dint move rite away. Dint no what to do ware to go. The loyer pointd.

Streetcar stop is there on the corner he said. Good by.

He shook my hand and went back in.

I never saw him agane.

I SENT JADEN
AN OTHER TEXT

AND WATED. NOTHING. I dint no any other possy numbers so I got on a streetcar for home. I dint no ware els to go. I got a text from Spencer— almost dun jackfish. Whatever that ment. I dint no what a jackfish was. Then gost town tomoro morning. I red it agane but dint understand the fish part. Unless jackfish was a place. Maybe that was it. Mayb it was the gost town. I sent him a text back but it dint go thru. Error said my sell phone. I tryd agane. And agane. Error. Error. I lookd up wen the driver calld out a street name I dint no.

Inside the streetcar evrything lookd norml. Ads for movys and pills and sad babys and a pull cord over the door. But outside was differnt. I dint no the street names or the stores. We past a restront and a church and a park with a glass house in the middl. Weerd eh? House made of glass. A minit later we came to the end of the rode and the streetcar turnd like a car. I dint no they cud do that but this 1 turnd rite and kept going. What to do? What to do? Dad says wen your lost stay ware you r and sum 1 will find you. But what about now? If I stayed ware I was I wud keep moving. That was rong wasnt it?

I calld Moms sell phone and home. I got the voys saying pleas leev your name and hung up. I never no what to say to the voys. I dint want to say help me Im lost. Id sound like a littl kid.

I countd parking meters. I dint no what els to do. They were on both sides of the street so I was up to 20 22 24 in no time.

Moving moving. What to do? What to do? We turnd agane. Left. This streetcar was like a dodjem. Not so many restronts now. The stores were closed. Sum of the street lites were on and sum wernt. The windo was open. I cud hear the sound of the metal weels on the metal rales. A singing sound.

No more meters. I went up to the driver and ast ware he was going. He told me a name but I dint no ware that was. I ast if it was any ware near Tecumsee and he shook his head. Your on the rong car— Tecumsee is back there he said.

The weels sang on the rales.

Let me off! I said. Man O man O. I was going away from home. Evry second I was farther and farther away. Let me off! I said agane. Let me off! Let me off!!

I got so upset that the driver stoppd in the middl of a block and opend the doors. I jumpd onto the rode and almost got run over by a littl green car. The driver had his mouth open wide.

Shut up! I said to him. Shut up! Shut up! Shut up!

I pounded the hood of the car and walkd away slow.

The partments on my side of the street were ugly and squashd and no 1 cared what was in them. Like boxes at the back of the closet. Windos with bords on them. Close hanging over ralings.

It was 9:10 by my sell phone. I was breething better now that I wasnt going the rong way.

I was stoppd and sum 1 wud find me. And sum 1 did—an old raggy guy. But he cudnt help me cuz he dint no ware he was ether. I ast him and he pointd at the sky and at the ground and then shook his head. So I gave him a loony and he wandered away smelling like garbaj. Next past me was a girl with a baby. I ast ware I was and she laffd and kept going. No I meen it ware am I? I yelld. She went into 1 of the box places pushing her stroller.

A streetcar went past. It was weerd to see it coming around the corner tord me. On the front it said *MAIN*. I calld home agane but it was still the voys on the other end. I startd to jump up and down. I cud feel myself getting workd up agane. Like water on the stove. All the bubbls going up and up. Thats how my insides felt. My phone said *9:11*. Then *9:12*. Then *9:12* agane. I was talking out loud. I do that sum times. Come on I said. Come on come on.

My phone buzzd. Mom I thot. But it was Jaden.

Hi! I shoutd.

Bunny?

Did you get my text?

Yah he said. Ware r you?

I dont no!

Were cruzing around he said. The jim is off limits. Cobra is at home and the rest of us r in Jellos car. You shud be here. You want to come along?

Yah! I said. But you have to find me.

Jaden said no problem. He ast what I cud see and I told him about the streetcar that said *MAIN* and the box houses and he said the same as Dad—stay ware you r and weel get you he said.

I stared at the store across the street. There was used stuff for sale in the windo—a thing to put your close in with drawers and a meer on top and a trumpet hanging on a string and stacks of DVDs. The windo had bars across it. The sun was down but there was still lite in the sky. I cud here car doors and music. A siren rising and falling a long way away. City things. I cud here the same things outside my place.

I thot about that. I dint want to be here but did I want to go home? I did and I dint. What wud I do at home? What was home any way? My famly? My stuff?

Huh.

I dint notice the 2 guys until they came rite up and ast for my shoos.

What? I said.

Your shoos. Take them off said the big guy with the cigar and hat.

Why?

Cuz there good 1s. And you dont belong here. Take them off.

He was blowing smoke up—like a chimny. The other guy was behind me now. He movd sneeky and sideways.

We were standing under a street lite and it came on just then.

I seen that befor said the cigar guy.

He was staring at my arm.

A guy in my range at Millhaven had that 15 on his chest. Striped like that. Thot he was cool as any thing but he was crap. You seen that 15 befor Dixon?

The other guy made wisper sounds from behind me. I dint no what he was saying. Sum thing rong with the way he talkd. I tryd to look at both guys at the same time. Dixon pulld a long stick out of his pocket and slappd it on his hand. Not a stick from a tree but like a club. The big guy threw away his cigar and made his hands into fists. These 2 reely wantd my shoos. I thot about xplaning about them being a birthday present but I new they wudnt care. I wonderd how much the club wud hurt. Probly a lot.

What a mess. It was bad being lost but this was worse. Things can always get worse. But they can get better 2 and they did rite then. A car pulld up to ware we were standing—old car about a block long with a black body and white top. Jaden was leening out the windo. Hey Bunny he said and I said Hey back. Befor the car stoppd he was on the sidewalk and so was Xray. Doors swinging. The car rumbld like it was about to spit. Jello got out the driver side and Snocone with him so now there were 4 of them on the sidewalk with me. And the other guys were gone. I dint see them go but they were hurrying down the walk to the next bilding block place. The door swung shut behind them.

What was that about? said Snocone.

My shoos I said.

Huh?

Jello was all reddy in the car. Jaden was shaking his head. Man Bunny we leev you alone for a minit you get in a mess.

I got in the back with Jaden and Xray. Jello made a U turn and we rored away.

If that cop Don was there Id say to him told you so. They do care.

WE DROVE
AROUND

PLACES I NEW and places I dint. Down along
the river to the lake and then across town under
the xpress way ware there were pot holes and
hobos and the CNE and then back up thru streets
I new with houses and partments and parkd cars
and dark lanes and trees. Streetcar tracks made us
bump up and down. Music playd. Bildings leend on
each other. Smells of garbaj and summer nites. Peepl
around—lots of them. Jello slowd down wenever
we past a park and we all stared out the windos.
I dint no what I was looking for but I stared all rite.

1 time we drove into a parking lot and rolld reel slow past a car with guys sitting on it and they all stared at us and we stared at them. Our music was loud and so was theres. We drove away still staring.

Raders? said Jaden.

Raders said Snocone.

Hate those guys said Xray.

Jello got a phone call that made him sware. He lissend and nodded and swore sum more. Yah Ill tell them he said. He threw the phone down on the seat next to him.

That was Cobra he said. Deels off.

He turnd up the radio. We were on a twisty street with big houses.

Jaden was shaking his head so I did 2. I dint want him to think I dint care.

This is bad news rite? I wisperd.

Yah.

The car went skid round a corner. Jaden bumpd into me.

Deel was to pay for the jim said Jaden. Were behind on the rent. If we dont do the deel we dont get the money. They kick us out of the jim. Morgan has no ware to live. We have no ware to hang out. Jello is traning for UFC. Without the jim he has no ware to trane.

Too bad I said.

Jello was zooming down the rode. There were speed bumps and the car went *bang bang* wen we hit them. The lite went from yello to red. We dint slow down. *Bang.*

Hey said Snocone from the passenger seat. Hey Jello!

Bang.

The lite was red. Jello held on to the weel tite. Snocone yelld at him to stop. Jaden put his hand on my arm. I was counting my breths agane. I cud feel the air going in 2 3 out 2 3. There was a crack in the wind sheel—*zig zag zig*. At the last minit Jello slammd on the brakes but we dint stop. It was 2 late and we went skid and kept going. We were rite at the lite now and there were cars going across the street in front of us. Jello spun the weel and our car went round in haff a circle so we were facing back the way we came. And now—now we stoppd.

Jello turnd in his seat.

Shut up! he yelld. Evry 1 just shut up—OK?

We went back the way we came. Jaden shook his head. I was trying to think what this reminded me of.

They talkd about things I dint understand. Points and numbers that dint meen a thing. Ware we cud get money. Who wud by our stuff off us. How much time we had. Not much. Thats my point said Jello a few times. My hole point. We got to move now. We need money by next week. Thats wen the rents do. We got to find a deel. We got stuff to sell—we got to sell it. Got to find sum 1 to sell it to. Any 1 thinks differnt you can get out of the car now—OK?

No 1 said any thing for a bit. Then Xray said he dint trust the Angels.

Yah I said.

Well I dont trust those Raders said Snocone. Or the Sonix.

Who we going to deel with then? ast Jello.

I wish Scratch wasnt in Torrents said Jaden. Wens he back?

We were over by Hi Park—trees on our left there branches full of darkness. Stars on top like salt on french frys. Old timey. Spooky. Kind of sad.

Torrents? I wispered to Jaden. You meen where my brother is? Cuz hes not there now.

The lite changed. We took off like a sling shot and I thot about being in the car with Mom and Dad upset about sum thing so that there feelings— the upset feelings—wud spill over the back seat. Id ast Mom why she was fiting with Dad and she wud say they never fot—that this was a free xchange of ideas. Spencer wud be sitting beside me reeding a comic and rolling his eyes.

One time we were on our way to the cottage and Mom almost hit a squirrl and Dad told her to go slower and she said if he dint like her driving he cud get out of the car and not go to the cottage. He said that sounded good to him and she told him to watch out. Dont you dare Jerry O'Toole she said.

Thats what it was like now—Snocone getting mad at Jellos driving and Jello telling us we cud get out of the car.

They were talking about me. Jaden was saying I must have lernd fiting wen I was inside and Jello was saying I was pretty good but not as good as him.

His ink is fresh said Snocone. How long he bin 15?

Thats what I want to no said Xray.

Hes rite here—why dont you ast? said Jaden.

We were passing a hotel. The sine was lit up but there were letters missing. Park sum thing and then Arms.

So what about it white boy? said Xray. Scratch and Jello and me bin 15 a long time—gonna be 15 a long time. What about you?

Silents. They were wating for me to talk.

Im 15 a hole year I said. Then Ill be 16.

There was a small soft minit and then they all startd to laff.

What did you meen about your brother? Jaden ast me.

Huh?

Just now you were saying about him not being in Torrents. What you meen?

Hes not in Torrents any more I said. Hes on his way to sum place calld Jackfish.

Jello pulld off to the side of the rode and stoppd. The sine said *No Parking* but he stoppd any way and turnd around in his seat. Snocone 2—they both stared at me from the front.

I think its a place I said.

I got out Spencers text about the gost town. Snocone found Jackfish on a map on his sell phone and Jello calld Cobra and they had a long talk. Xray and Snocone were saying do you beleev this guy and Jaden was smiling and saying way to go Bunny. I dint no why any of this was happening but I smiled cuz they liked sum thing I did.

I wonderd if Spencer new all these guys were thinking about him.

✤

Mom lookd up from her book. Your home late she said. What have you bin doing?

Racing over speed bumps in a car I said.

She shook her head. Still joking Bunny. I spose it was a pleece car?

No that was befor I said.

She scrunchd up her face and lookd at me.

You wernt drinking beer were you? You no what weve told you.

No.

I went upstares to put goop on my tatoo. 2 days Id had it and it seemd like part of me.

I DREEMD

I WAS RUNNING on the cottage rode. Summer green beside me and the rode in front and I cud here my breth in 1 out 2 in 1 out 2. I was alone and then I herd feet behind me and Spencer and Mom and Dad went running by together. Spencer was watching a movy on his sell phone. Dad had his bandana. I yelld at them to stop but they dint. Then more feet and Ed from my class went past me and Grampa was running with him and pointing at Eds arrow tatoo and they ran away from me and I was breething in out in out and my arm hurt. Nun of this seemd weerd in the dreem not even the Grampa part.

But I felt bad until the possy came running up to me—Xray moning and Jello with his tummy hanging over his pants and Snocone looking back at me like he did from the front seat of the car. Cobra with his hand on my sholder and Jaden with a big smile. They said hi and we ran together and I dint feel so bad xept for my arm that was still hurting and xept for my breething that was so loud. It was like I was breething my own name. In 1 out 2 Bun ny Bun ny in out in out Bun ny.

Bun ny!

Moms voys. I woke up. She was bending over me wispering in my ear.

Bun ny!

Yah?

Shhh! she said. Theres sum 1 down stares.

I sat up. Mom kept her face near my ear. Wares your sell phone? she ast. I want to call the pleece but my phones in the kitchen.

I dint understand rite away. Whos down stares? Is it Spencer?

No. No. Shhh. Lissen Bunny I just want your sell phone.

Is it Dad?

No.

Is it—?

Shhh!

She was wispering but there was that Jeez Bunny! sound in her voys.

I herd a clunk from down stares. Jaden or 1 of the other guys from the possy. I no its stupid but thats what I thot. They were in my dreem and now I thot they were in my house. I went down and turnd on the lite and there was this guy but he wasnt 1 of my frends. He had a ski hat pulld down with eye holes so I cudnt see his face. And a nife in his hand.

Wares your money? he said. I want your money.

I new the nife. It was ours. Thats why I wasnt scared. Its hard to be scared of your own stuff. I membered that nife from forever. In the sink. In the drawer. In Dads hands. It was part of my house like the couch or the TV remot or the car keys. Wud you be scared of sum 1 waving your car keys at you? Rite.

Get out! yelld Mom. She was on the stares. I phond the pleece! she yelld. There on there way! Get out of my house!

I thot your phone was down here Mom I said.

Shut up Bunny!

She was shaking. She was scared. Mom was scared.

I member Morgan showing me how to kick in case of a nife fite. I got reddy to kick. But I dint have to.

Your 15 the guy said to me.

Yah.

He took a step back. O he said and agane smaller— like o.

He droppd the nife and a garbaj bag he had in his other hand and ran past me to the kitchen and out the back door. And that was that. I never saw him agane. I dont even no why Im putting this in— I gess cuz of Moms phone the next day.

She came all the way down stares now and gave me a hug. She was shaking. OK I said. OK.

He said you were 15 she said. Did he meen your tatoo?

Yah. It scared him off.

Well at leest its good for sum thing she said.

We checkd over the down stares. The windo in the back door was broke. I went on the porch and lookd round. It wasnt morning yet but the sky over on the left was differnt. The nite was blurry like sum 1 was trying to rub it out. The moon was a tiny slice floting over the shado of the trees. I herd the xpressway humming in the distance. I shiverd and went in.

MY RITING HAND IS HURTING

SO ILL SPEED UP. Moms phone was in the bag the guy droppd and it broke so she used my phone to call a guy to fix the back door. He came with a tool kit and a smile. Sorry to intrupt your morning he said and went rite to work.

Dad says TV is a trap and a waste of time but Mom puts it on wen hes not around. The news woman had big hair and a big micro phone. She said sum thing about American gangsters and the streets of Trono and guns and drugs. She shook her head at us to show how awful it was. This is

Lisa Cook reporting from 52 Divishun she said. Wen the camera pulld back there was the statu of the kid pulling the wagon.

What do you call that thing? I ast Mom.

What?

That thing on the wagon—that triangl thing. What is it?

Peer amid she said.

O.

The door fixer was dun. He took Moms check with a smile. Im sorry for your trubbl mam he said. You have a grate day. He left closing the door behind him. What a guy. Came rite away and did his job. Strong hands white teeth no fuss. What wud the world be if evry 1 was like him? Wud it be perfect?

❋

Mom had stuff 2 do down town. She ast did I want 2 go with her but I dint cuz I was meeting Jaden.

Then I want you close to home she said. After what happend last nite I want 2 no ware you are.

O.

Will you do that for me Bunny? Stay inside or close by?

I took a deep breth. Yah I said.

But I dint meen it.

✳

The woman on the streetcar wudnt stop talking. She had 1 of those ear kind of sell phones with wires hanging and she went on and on about a party last nite ware sum 1 did this amazing thing she dint beleev it and how bisy she was today and all the time she was waving her arms round. Her voys was like sizzers. Other peepl were staring 2 wishing she wud stop talking or get off the streetcar or dy. I cud see the wire going from her ear down the back of her shirt and coming out the bottom—and I saw it wasnt pluggd into any thing. She was saying I no Im just awful and o my god your sooooooo rite and all the time the wire was dangling and she dint even no. Funny eh? I was going to say your frend cant here you but the streetcar came to my stop and I got off. The woman was still talking to no 1.

Jaden was wating outside a park down the bottom of 19 Street.

I shudnt be here I said. I told my mom I wud stay home.

So who nose ware you are? he said.

No 1—xept you.

Thats good.

It is? Does your gramma no ware you are?

Cors not. We smiled—2 guys lying to there famly.

You reddy to pick up the stuff? said Jaden.

Stuff I said.

The deels on agane and this is our end of it. Stuff. You no—*bang bang!*

Rite I said. *Bang bang.*

We walkd thru candy rappers and gees and the smell of the lake. A squirrl stared at me from on top of a garbaj can. He had black button eyes and a nod like hello. I wonderd what his name was. Zeke mayb. Zeke the squirrl. He had a donut in his paws and he took a littl bite and held it out to me. I shook my head no thanks.

Bunny! This way!

Rite I said. Later Zeke.

The park had a slide and a sand box and a bunch of trees and a hill. Up on top of the hill was a statu of— I dunno—a thing. A blob with a curvy line. There were 2 picnic tables up by the statu and evry 1 was sitting on the tables. Cobra was there and Snocone and Jello and Xray and Morgan. And a guy I dint no—thin guy bent like a paper clip with a smoke hanging out his mouth.

Cobra stood up wen he saw me. We did the 15 thing—pound and xplode.

Thanks he said.

Huh?

This guy he said to the others. This guy Bunny saved us.

They nodded. Snocone lookd unhappy but he nodded 2. Wo Bunny! said Jello. He was pink today— big shirt with buttons down the front.

I stood in the middl of the picnic tables and Cobra put his hands on both my sholders. He told evry 1 there about Spencer and Al Capoli going 2 Jackfish and how Scratch and Hobo drove all nite 2 Jackfish 2 and now evry 1 was in Jackfish and the deel was on agane. I dint no why they cared so much about Spencer but they did and they were happy now and that was grate.

And the actress I said.

Huh? said Cobra.

Why Spencers in Jackfish I said. He has to get a kiss from an old lady—Gloria sum thing. It was my grampas idea. Like my cuzzen DJ going to Africa and my tatoo. We got nvelopes I said.

No 1 said any thing. From up here the lake smell was stronger. I cud see a bit of it thru the trees and houses—a spit of water flashing in the sun. With the sun on it the water lookd silver not blu.

Cobra got a phone call. Hey Julius he said. And walkd away from us to here better. The paper clip guy came over and gave me the 15 sine.

Beens talk he said.

They do? I said.

What they call me he said. Cuz Im skinny you no? And my reel names Jack. Like Jack and the beens talk.

The cigaret stayd in his mouth moving up and down wen he was talking. He sounded like gravel.

Bunny I said. Like Bunny.

Cobra had to go rite away and he took Morgan with him. Befor he went he pointd to his littl brother.

You get into the lock up—OK Jaden? Jello can drive you. Take enuff guys to carry the stuff. You member ware it is rite? Good. Thanks.

Jaden smiled.

Cobra was still on the phone. Dammit Julius he said going down the hill. Dammit why they need me?

Whos Julius? I ast Jaden.

Thats Uncle Julius—our loyer. Dint you see him last nite at the pleece stashun? I told him about you.

Hes your uncle?

Yah. He nose evrything.

Well he sure dint want to no any thing more from me I said.

Zeke the squirrl came back and stood with his paws hanging in front like he was begging. I found a candy in my pocket and got down on my nees. Held out the candy. Zeke took it and ran off and an other squirrl came up looking xactly the same. I wonderd if mayb he was Zeke or if he just lookd like him. And then I thot it dint matter who he was he cud still have a candy xept I dint have any more candy. Tuff luck Zeke I said. Wen I got up the guys were staring at me.

Were going to pick up the stuff now Bunny said Jaden.

Stuff? I said. You meen like—*bang bang?*

Thats what I meen!

Beens put out his fist and I punchd it. Snocone had a sour xpreshun like he was drinking milk from the back of the frij witch is a bad idea. Trust me.

JADEN NEW WARE TO GO

BUT HE WASNT OLD ENUFF to drive so he sat in the front beside Jello. Snocone dint come with us and ether did Morgan. So it was me in the back with Beens and Xray. Beens was next to me. He smelld like candy canes. We drove on the xpressway for a bit and then got off it. Jaden told Jello to take this exit and we went down. Turn here he said and we turnd. Go strate. Turn here. And here. Jello did what Jaden said.

You sure this is the rite place? said Xray. I never bin down here. I never herd of any 15 stuff down here. You Jello? Beens? You no this place?

Nope said Jello hands on the weel.

Beens gruntd no.

You sure its the rite place kid? said Xray.

Cobra took me here said Jaden.

We were in a strange broken part of the city—xpressway on 1 side of us and lake on the other—driving on dirt and bumps and dead grass and the car jiggling up and down past hobos and see gulls and bildings with no roofs and piles of trash and shopping carts and ovens and things like that. Past broken fences keeping no 1 out of no ware. I cud smell the lake and the trash and sum thing burning and sum thing rotten. We jiggld up to a sine that said *LOK ALL* and an arrow pointing to the rite. Follow that said Jaden.

LOK ALL was 1 place ware the fence workd. We stoppd and wated for the guy to open the gate—*chinka chinka chinka.* It pulld side ways and we drove ahead slow. There was a line of garajs with oranj doors. The 1 at the far end was ours. Jello stoppd the car and we all got out.

I dint no about this place Jello said. Did you guys?

No 1 ever tells me any thing said Xray.

Beens shook his head.

Jaden opend the locker with a key from round his neck. The door went up and I saw the stack of boxes sitting on the stone floor.

The stuff.

They lookd like regular cardbord boxes to me— like youd find at the no frills store—but evry 1 was going Wow! and O yah! so I said it 2.

All rite! Stuff! I said.

Jaden punchd my sholder.

The riting on the side of the boxes said *Sum thing Sum thing Car Parts*. It also said *Handl With Care*. It also said *China*. I dint have time to reed it all befor we were loding them into the car. That dint take long and Jello closed the trunk and we were dun.

We stood in front of the garaj and nodded at each other.

So the deels on said Jello. R we reddy? Is evry 1 reddy?

Yah we said.

Come on louder! I said is evry 1 reddy? You reddy Jaden? Xray? Beens? You reddy Bunny?

Yah!

We got back in the car. This time Xray got in front. I sat in between Jaden and Beens and took a deep breth in—Hahhh. And held it. It was good to be hanging out with these guys.

I let out the breth—Ahhhh.

The trip back was reel slow cuz we were riding low. The bottom of the car scraped wen we went over any bump. I cud hear the boxes rattling in the trunk.

What kind of car parts r they? I ast. The boxes r pretty hevvy. Do they have like tires or mufflers or steering weels or what in them?

Jaden poked me. Your funny he said.

Uh huh.

I wasnt joking. But I dint say so.

We were riding along Lake Shore past trees and big houses and stores that sold things for a dollar. The next sine was Mimico Street. So thats ware we were.

We stoppd in front of a partment bilding wating for the lite. Xray new the bilding. He was talking about all the things rong with it. The water dint work and the elvaters dint work and there were bugs and noys and other things and after a wile I stoppd lissening. Across the street a woman was walking a lizard. Thing was as long as her arm. It movd slow and careful—one leg at a time. A reel lizard. It lookd old like from befor time startd. I pokd Jaden.

Hey! Cool! he said. The lite changd and we drove on.

Beens leend over to me.

You white he said.

Yah.

Never sat next to a white guy in a car he said.

I have I said. Lots of times.

He laffd. Jaden herd me and he laffd 2. So I gess it was funny.

A motor bike passd us on the inside. *Vroom.* An other 1 on the outside. *Vroom.* 2 bikes. The riders had that Å on there jackets. They rode ahead of us side by side.

Angels I said.

Yah said Jello.

He drove. The Angels vroomd ahead of us on there bikes. Xray was talking about how his place dint work ether. The door dint open and the buzzer dint buzz and there were flys in the butter.

More vrooming. There was a bike beside us. A guy with a beerd stared into the car. 2 more bikes behind us. Xray stoppd talking. Jaden put his hand on my arm.

Do they no who we r? I ast.

O yah.

It was tents. I cud feel it. We drove like this for a wile bikes in front of us and behind us and beside us. No 1 talkd. I cud smell swet like after jim class. I was counting my breths. Finally I leend across Jaden and stuck my arm out the windo.

Go away! I yelld at the biker.

Beens pulld me back in. Jaden wisperd to me to shut up.

You crazy? said Jello. You want to get in a fite with stuff in the trunk?

The Angel beside us stared in. I stared out. A block later all the bikes vroomd off down a side street and the rode around us was empty. I cud feel evry 1 relaxing. We kept going past 10 Street and 11 and Jello fartd reel loud witch made us all laff. Xray startd moning about the smell.

I turnd to Jaden. Angels r still the bad guys rite? I said. So why cant I yell at them?

Member the deel with them? We need to be nice for now Cobra said.

O yah the deel I said.

He smiled. He cud have bin all like Jeez Bunny but he wasnt.

I forgot the deel I said to Beens who shook his head but he was kinda smiling 2.

Tomoro said Jello. Deels today so you can yell at the Angels tomoro.

We turnd in at the Burger King on 16 Street and the Lake Shore.

There r the guys said Jaden.

THEY CRAMMD
INTO THE CAR

AND WE WENT TO Snocone's house. I dint see ware that was cuz the back seat was full of legs and arms and behinds after Snocone and Morgan and Bonesaw piled in. I dint no he was Bonesaw then just a big guy with a bald head standing in the parking lot with bags of food but I met him later wen I spilld on him. Any way evry 1 was shouting and talking and Jello was saying watch out for the gear shifter and the car was smelling like french frys—you no how it does—and we stoppd with a jerk and Jello said get out get out and we did. It was a house with a stroller on the lon and we went inside and there was a lady in the kitchen holding a baby and making fart noys on the babys tummy with her lips you no what I meen? Wen she saw us all she stoppd making noys and the baby stoppd laffing.

Hi Mom said Snocone. Hi Lucy.

I dint beleev it was his mom. She lookd like his sister. Not just yung but weerd yung. My mom cud be Snocones moms mom. Snocones gramma. Witch wud make me Snocones—I dont no. Any way she was yung. What Im saying.

Hello Arthur she said. Hows my boy?

Snocone dint anser—he went down stares and so did Xray Jello and Beens. Morgan stoppd to say hi to Snocones mom. He was older than us but not like a dad older. More like a big brother. Now I saw he cud be a dad. He held out his french frys and she took sum and gave 1 to the baby who droppd it. Morgan ast how she was doing and pokd the baby and the baby went *bla* like they do. It was like he was her boyfrend.

They were talking about me down stares. I herd them. Snocone was saying but hes so dum and I new he ment me. There were laffs and sum 1 ast if I was for reel. Jello said I was fast and that was for reel.

Jaden told evry 1 to shut up and that I new enuff to save the deel and that Cobra thot I was OK. Wen I got down stares they were talking about sum thing els. Jello threw a burger at me and I cot it. See he said to the guy next to him. What did I tell you? Hes fast.

The down stares had white walls and a brown rug and there were chairs and sofas and TVs. There was music playing from sum ware. I cudnt find a place to sit so I ate standing up witch is wen I spilld on the guy I dint no—I was standing next to him and I spilld ketchup out the back of my burger. You ever dun that? And it landed on his bald head and I said oops and Jaden laffd. I tryd to wipe the ketchup but it dint come off and the bald guy jumpd up and swung his fist at me. I cot it in my hand and said I was sorry and evry 1 was crowding round. He went to the bathroom and wen he came back I said sorry agane and he shook his head and said whatever. Thats wen I found out he was Scratchs brother and his name was Bonesaw. He told me my tatoo was a lot like his brothers. He wantd to no ware I did it and I said the place up on Lake Shore. And he said no the candl—ware did that happen? I said the same place.

Roxy was her name I said. She was bald like you.

A bunch of us were talking about spooky things—
dead guys coming back to hont you and like that.

I saw sum 1 after he was dead I said. I was thinking
of Grampa on the TV at the loyers offis.

A gost? said Beens all gravelly.

Kind of I said.

We were finishd our lunch. I was sitting on the
floor with my back to the wall. Jaden was next to
me and Beens was on a couch. He sat up.

Did the gost talk to you?

Yah for a long time. He was xplaning stuff I said.

The others were staring at me now. Snocone turnd
away from the video game. Bonesaw was frowning
like he dint beleev me but he was watching 2.

What was the gost xplaning?

Like my task—what Im sposed to do I said.

Seeryus?

Jadens eyes were wide.

You guys think Im dum I said. Well I am but
seeryus things happen 2 dummys 2. I saw a gost of
my grampa and he gave me a task. And now Im here.

Evry 1 was staring now and saying weerd.

Did you see the gost agane? said Jaden.

I saw his coffin. But that was befor.

Bonesaw shudderd. They startd talking about music insted of gosts and I stoppd lissening cuz I dont no much about that. Snocones mom came down with Morgan. She startd to pick up the mess. Morgan put the baby on the floor and it rolld around.

Sum 1 shoutd Jackson! and evry 1 startd laffing. I thot they ment Mikel Jackson but no. Wen I ast they laffd at me 2 and turnd away. They were talking about sum 1 els named Jackson. O well.

Who did you think they ment? I ast Jello who was sitting near me.

Huh?

You lookd up wen they said Jackson.

Did not he said.

Sure you did.

Shut up.

His phone rang then.

Hey Cobra he said.

He pushd the phone into his ear and stared up at the seeling and lissend hard.

Yah we reddy to go he said. Jaden let us into the locker. The stuff is in the trunk of the caddy now.

Were at Snocones. Yah Bonesaws here 2. You herd from Scratch?

I was on the floor. Baby Lucy crawld over to me and put a hand on my arm. Her fingers were tiny and soft and kind of sticky. Ew. She got a funny look on her face. Like she was talking to sum 1 a long way off—like God or sum 1. Jello did 2. They both had the same look—staring at the seeling and talking to far away.

But you going to be there rite? said Jello.

He lissend sum more and said OK and By and put away his phone. We were all watching.

Deels on he told us. Cobra will meet us at the mall.

We made a huddl like in a football game—Jello in the middl and us facing in—and he xplaned what we were sposed to do and we made a 1 2 3 cheer and ran up stares.

I was next to Jello. Dont worry I told him. Itll be fine. The deel will work and then we can pay for the jim and you can keep traning.

What? he said.

Thats what we want rite?

He dint anser.

Morgan kissd Snocones mom and the baby Lucy good by. She slappd Morgans face with both hands left rite left and he smiled.

Sum 1 stinks he said.

Your rite said Snocones mom. O Lucy!

I was near by and I cud smell it 2. I new what Lucys faraway look ment now. She wasnt talking to God—she was pooping.

WE WERE ALL GOING TO THE MALL

CUZ THATS WARE THE DEEL was happening.
Cobra wantd the hole possy there just in case.
We dint trust those Angels and Buffalos in Torrents
and we dint trust them in Jackfish and we dint trust
them here. We just dint trust them.

Jaden and Snocone and Beens and me were on
the bus. The others were coming by car. Jaden and me
in the very back seat and Snocone and Beens sitting
sideways in the seats ahead. The sine on the front
of the bus said *SURE WAY*. That was the name of
the mall. Sure Way Gardens.

I wantd to no sum thing. If we dont trust them do they trust us? I ast.

Beens made a deep snorty sound.

No 1 trusts no 1 he said.

The bus went along a street calld Evans. Down a hill and up a hill past tire stores and donut shops and places with sines selling I dunno what. 1 of them said *Systems*. I wonderd what you got there? At a donut shop you get donuts. Whats a System?

We past a big restront and a big movy theeter and sum other big stores selling big things. Minded me of the gun in my pants.

Yah thats what I said. Gun. Jello ast if we were carrying and suddenly evry 1 was pulling out guns. Like it was a TV show down in Snocones basment—guys holding pistols and pointing them and checking that there were enuff bullets. Cool eh? And nives—Jaden had 1 that folded up and then snappd open.

Jello ast ware my pipe was.

Pipe?

You no—your gun.

So thats what a pipe was. I dint have 1.

My mom hates guns I said.

Jello thot that was funny. He took a pistol out of his pants and gave it to me. I said what about him? He told me not to worry and liftd his shirt to show me an other gun on the other side.

You no how to use it? he said.

Sure.

Evry 1 nose how to use a gun rite? Point and shoot. I must of killd 1000s of aliens and zombis. 1000s and 1000s. I put the gun in my pants like him. My shirt hung out over it. I lookd like me but felt funny.

Its loded said Jello. Dont shoot your balls off.

Balls. I laffd.

❋

The bus stoppd and sum oldys driftd in slow and blinky. A bossy woman in a red cap told them to find a seat find a seat find a seat. The bus startd up agane. The oldys sat with there white heads nodding like dolls as the bus bumpd along. 1 of the oldys ast if she cud stay standing up and look out the windo.

I want to see she said. Ill hold on tight I promise. I have a good grip.

She was a littl lady with bisy hands she rappd round a pole then unrappd then rappd agane. They were like 2 spiders on the ends of her arms.

No!

The bossy red cap pushd her in the nearest seat.

Stay there Dinty! she said. Ive had about enuff of you.

Dinty I thot. Funny name but it went with her. She was a dinty lady. Like crumpld and used but OK. Like how a dinty pale wud still hold water.

She glared up at the lady in the red cap.

Your such a not see said Dinty.

Jaden punchd my arm then leend forward and tappd Beens and Snocone.

We reddy? he said.

Snocone opend his fist and there was the 15 sine on his hand—the inside of his hand.

Im with the possy all the way he said.

Me 2 said Beens.

And me said Jaden.

And me I said.

Not just to be saying sum thing. I ment it. And me.

The bus bumpd up a big hill and round a bend. The mall was below us small and white with parkd cars all round. From up here the stores lookd like peaces of soap floting in the lake. The cars were the lake.

RAINY DAYS
AT THE COTTAGE

THEY PLAYD CARDS. 1 time Spencer and DJ and Webb I think and Anty Vicky were round the dining room table. Grampa saw me yonning and took me by the hand. Just me. We went to his work room and he showd me this sord. A reel 1 like at the museum. He let me touch it and pointd to the stain on the pointy end. Thats blud Bernard he said. He xplaned that he took the sord off a bad guy wen he was yung. The blud was from a good guy the bad guy was fiting and thats why Grampa never cleend the sord—cuz he wantd to member the good guy.

I ast him what the good guys name was and Grampa shook his head. I never met him he said.

So how do you no he was good? I ast him.

He was on my side he said.

And that was the good 1.

Yah.

How do you no?

Grampas teeth lookd yello wen he smiled. He said it was hard to xplane.

You just no he said. Your guys r the good guys. You feel it. Trust that feeling Bernard. Trust yourself.

OK I said.

He pickd up the sord. Pretty cool eh? Grampa with his white hair and sad smile staring out the windo. And the sord with the rusty blud on it and the rain running down the windo pane.

There was an ants nest in the corner of the work-room. Grampa got 2 cans of Raid and gave 1 to me. We sprayd the crap out of all those ants. Got you! he yelld. Dy you littl basterds. Dy! Made me laff.

I told Spencer this story that nite. Grampa likes you he said.

Even tho Im a dummy?

Even tho.

You shud of seen us bomming those ants I said.
Grampa was rite into it.

He flew bommers in the war Bun. Member what
Dad said—hes a killer.

Grampas a killer I said into the dark. Grampas a
killer. Grampas a killer.

Sum 1 from down the hall told me to shut up.

MY SIDE HURT.

THE BUS RUMBLD AND WEEZD under an xpressway. The sun came out for a second and hit me rite in the eye. East Mall Rode said the driver. East Mall Rode is next.

What you doing with that thing?

Snocone was frowning at me.

Nothing I said.

Put it away. Jeez.

I had the gun out staring at it. Blu gray color. A shape like my finger and thum wen I pretend to shoot only this wasnt pretend. I stuck it back in my pants.

Sorry.

Your crazy he said.

The bus rolld into the mall parking lot past the Sears store and the sport store. Past the white bricks and banners and parkd cars and fat peepl and strollers and hats. And bags. Evry 1 had a bag. The bags from the sport place were blu and the 1s from Sears were white. I kept count.

Sure Way said the bus driver. Sure Way Gardens.

The oldys were ahead of us. They movd off first with Red Cap bullying them along. Stay together til we get to the movy theeter she said. She kept close to Dinty—the oldy who wantd to see evrything.

Snocone had his phone out. Hi Jello he said. Yah. Yah. OK.

He put it away. Cobras with them he said. There on there way.

We walkd round the out side of the mall. Beens and Snocone were talking about what to do if there was trouble with the Angels or Buffalos. Snocone said we shud go in hard—reddy to fite. Show who we r so they no not to mess with us. Beens said sum thing I dint understand. Jaden turnd to me.

What do you think Bunny—if things go rong how shud we go in?

Together I said. Thats how. Cuz we r together.

We were round the front of the mall now. Cars parkd. Banners flappd. Clouds floted. We found a place to wate next to a low sement wall. My tatoo felt sticky. A lady came out of the mall with a white Sears bag. That made 44 of them to 36 blu.

I herd the *vroom vroom* sound in the distance. I new what it was and who.

Angels said Jaden.

Basterds said Snocone.

There were 4 bikers riding 2 and 2. They went round the parking lot leening over to turn. We watchd them ride out of site. Beens was thin and his head was big so it lookd like a lite on a pole. There checking the place out he said. Tell Cobra.

Snocone all reddy had his phone out.

Basterds r cheating he said. There here erly.

I wispered to Jaden. R we here erly?

Jaden nodded.

So were basterds 2 I said.

BEENS WENT INTO THE MALL

AND CAME OUT WITH COFFEES for him and
Snocone and cokes for me and Jaden. Snocone wasnt
much older than us but he got the grone up drink.
He liked that. I countd more blu and white bags.

We talkd about what made you strong. Not just
doing pushups and lifting wates but other stuff like
how you stuck with your frends and dint care what
any 1 els said. I told them about Grampa and having
a teem with you and that made you strong. Like he
had his own crew way back wen.

Who cares about your grampa? said Snocone.
What does your grampa no about being strong

and standing up for himself? What does he no about killing peepl?

Grampas a killer I said. He killd 100s and he hurt them 2—blu there arms off and there legs. He was strong all rite.

They stared at me.

100s? said Jaden.

At leest.

Thats what Dad said—100s at leest. Spencer and me were littl and we thot it was cool and Dad said no no the hole thing was aw full and evil. I ast if Grampa was evil and he said no that Grampa was fiting the not sees and they were evil. And then it was bed time.

A girl walkd past with her mom. She was about as old as me. Thin and pretty with sunglasses and hair pild up and tall shoos making her taller. Beens ast Jaden what he thot. That sisters pretty hot eh? Dint you think so Snocone? Bunny?

Shes hot all rite said Snocone.

Hot I said.

Jaden punchd me. I punchd him back. Beens sippd his coffee. The girl and her mom got in there car and drove away.

Jaden and I climed on the sement wall and startd walking up and down. I was thinking about the hot girl.

Cud I call her a sister? I ast.

Who? said Jaden.

Beens calld her a sister cuz shes black I said. And I was wondering if I cud call her a sister 2. Cuz shes still black even wen Im talking about her.

No.

No shes not black?

No you cant call her sister. Shes not your sister. Your white.

Is she your sister?

Yes.

He was so sure.

But shes still hot rite? I said.

The sun was out agane. Shining down it made things hard to look at. Why dint I have sunglasses? But I dint. Jaden stood on the wall with his hands out. I cud see the gun bump under his shirt.

Im glad your here Bunny he said.

Me 2.

You and me well stick together.

Yah.

The parking lot had poles with letters on them—
A B F like that. Jellos big black and white car pulld
into a free spot under the M. Cobra and Jello and
Morgan and what was his name got out and stood
round the car with there hands like this. Tuff.

Deel time. We movd closer—behind a van with
a dent in the side. I cud see a baby seat inside the van
with a Sponj Bob doll. You no Sponj Bob with the big
eyes and the skinny littl arms. Hes funny.

Angels were giving us money so we cud keep the
jim. I wonderd what we were giving them.

Vroom. The Angels were here. They rord round
the car. Round Cobra and Morgan and Jello and
Bonesaw—that was the name I forgot. Jello had a sell
phone up to his ear. Head turning to follow the bikes.

Basterds said Snocone.

Ware r the guys from Buffalo? said Beens.

Jaden put his hand in his shirt feeling for the gun.

The sky was the sky.

The bikes made farting noys wen they stoppd.
The Angel in front had a black beerd and vest like
a pirate. I new him from watching the TV news with
Mom that time. Cobra and Morgan were leening on
our car. I thot about Morgan kissing Snocones mom.

And teeching me to fall. The pirate Angel sat on his bike with his arms across his chest.

Wares the guys from Buffalo? Beens said agane.

Basterds said Snocone.

The Angels were wating. We were wating. I cud feel the wating like evry 1 was holding there breth together. I wonderd about evry 1 in the world holding there breth and what wud happen wen we all let it out.

I wonderd who Jello was talking to on the phone.

A dad came up to us. He was waring shorts and flip flops and carrying a littl kid in his arms. The kids hair was xploding around her head. Shorts. Brown legs. Littl toes in sandals.

Mine! said the kid. Mine! She was pointing at the van.

Snocone went close to the dad.

Were bisy here he said. Go away.

Dad took a step back. Uh he said.

Daddy! said the girl.

Uh.

He took an other step back and turnd. The top of a white bag stuck out of his shorts pocket. That made 76.

No! said the girl. Daddy! No! Go home. Go home!

A black SUV slid to a halt in front of the bikers. It had fat bumpers and head lites like eyes staring. A white guy stuck his head out the front windo.

1 of yous named Cobra? he shoutd. Im looking for a guy named Cobra and a guy named Zeke. Got sum thing for yous.

He said his words funny.

Guys from Buffalo! said Beens.

No more breth holding. The deel was going down now. Be reddy for any thing said Snocone in a low voys.

Jaden was staring across the hood of the van and biting his lip.

Any thing I thot. Any thing.

The baby girl and her dad were walking tord the mall. She was kicking and he was holding on tite.

Jello put away his sell phone. The SUV swung into a parking spot and the guy from the front ran around and opend the back door.

GUY CLIMING OUT OF THE SUV WAS OLDER THAN US

NOT LIKE MORGAN OR COBRA but reel old like Dad. Weerd to have this deel going on with your dad eh? He shook hands with the Angel pirate and said hi kid you must be Zeke. Im Bobby. Then he did it with Cobra only he dint call him kid. Im Bobby he said. He dint shout but he was loud enuff to here. He said he workd for Mr Wings in Buffalo and that Mr Wings wud of come himself but that he had a littl rat problem he was deeling with and sent him insted.

So lets do this he said.

I was reddy for any thing but I had to poke Jaden.

He talks funny I wisperd. His name came out Babby did you here?

Lets go you guys! said Snocone.

Jello was waving at us. Zeke the biker was waving 2 and the Buffalos were climing out of the suv. So there we all were around the M pole of the parking lot—our possy and the Buffalos and Angels. The Buffalos all wore soots and shiny sunglasses so there eyes lookd like meers. Morgan and Xray had the trunk of Jellos car open and they were taking out the boxes of car parts. 1 of the Angels took a nap sack off the back of his bike. Jaden poked me.

That guy he wispered.

Holding the nap sack? With the black gloves?
Yah.

Bobby was talking about Al Capoli. Al Capoli this and that. What he wantd to do to Al Capoli. What Rocko was doing to Al Capoli rite now.

Cobra hookd his finger at me like come here.

Me? I pointd at myself. He nodded.

The Buffalo guy stoppd talking wen he saw me.

Whos the white kid?

This is Bunny said Cobra.

Bunny with the tatoo. White bunny in a black gang. Yous do things funny up in Canada said Bobby.

Bunnys the 1 who found Al Capoli said Cobra. His brother phond from Jackfish.

Jackfish!

Bobby spat the word. Dont talk to me about Jackfish! he said. Mr Wings is there now. He keeps trying to call only he cant get thru on account of theres no what do you call it up there. What do you call it?

He lookd at me.

I dunno I said.

Well hes there. Finally. Do yous no how far away that podunk town is? Do yous no?

Far I said.

12 ours! To drive from 1 podunk town to an other podunk town it takes 12 ours! Thats the problem with Canada. Place is 2 big. And after Mr Wings and the boys take care of that rat Al Capoli they have to drive all the way back to Buffalo thru all those podunk towns. What?

I tryd to stop laffing.

Whats so funny now white rabbit? said Bobby.

Evry 1 went shhhh for a bit and I cud here banners flapping and sirens going *beep bo beep bo* and see gulls saying gimme.

Bobby wasnt happy about me laffing at him. He was old as Dad but not like him. You can laff at Dad. 1 time he was so mad he was spitting and cudnt talk rite and Spencer startd spitting 2 and they ended up laffing together for a long time.

Podunk I told Bobby. Podunk is funny.

And then evrything went rong and nothing was funny any more. Pleece cars were coming at us across the parking lot. 1 2 4 6. More. 8 9. They came from all over. I cudnt count them. The sirens were loud—*beep bo beep bo!* Lots of things happend reel fast—like Bobby calling us rats and jumping into the SUV and driving it rite into a pleece car. *Smash.* And Jello with his hands in the air saying dont shoot. And Angels vrooming away with pleece cars after them. And Jaden grabbing me and saying come on. We ran tord a crowd of screeming peepl and they made room for us and we went thru and into the mall. Behind me I cud here sirens and brakes and smashing and popping noys. I ast Jaden about the deel and he shook his head.

Its over he said. Cops found out. Were all dead.

O.

I dint say any more. We went past stores selling close and toys and more close and books. Mall stuff you no? Evrything was norml and yet not. Music playing peepl shopping and Jaden crying.

There there I said.

Stupid eh? There there. What does that even meen?

He wiped his face. You see what happend to my brother? he ast.

No.

Sure Way Mall goes in loops and you come back to the middl or you can go a differnt loop. Wen we saw the Angel with the nap sack Jaden swore and took the other loop to walk away from him.

Whats with you and that guy? I ast.

Dont you member him?

No.

Well I do.

We came to the fish tanks. I always like to look at them. I pointd the black fish out to Jaden. See? I said. They have these fluffy fins so they look like storm clouds floting.

No time Bunny.

Rite rite.

Next doors we came to had a crowd round them shuffling not going outside. We joind them. Sum girls were checking us out. About our age or mayb yunger. 1 was kinda fat.

You guys here whats going on? she said. There was a gun fite in the mall. Like gangs shooting each other. No ones allowd to go home and theres cops wating rite outside that door there! Isnt it xiting! she said. My moms watching on the news and like freaking out!

She smiled at Jaden.

My names Kira whats yours?

Her frends were staring at us all this time and now they draggd her away wispering and looking back at us. Then Kira gave a yell and they all startd running.

I dint get it but Jaden did.

Those girls will tell the cops about us he said.

Huh?

They no who we r. Come on! And cover your arm.

My—O.

HAFF WAY ROUND
A LOOP

WE PAST A BATHROOM and there was Snocone
looking out—just his head. Jaden pulld me after him.
Snocone was pacing up and down swaring.

Who did it? he said. Who set us up?

Did what?

How did the cops no about the deel? How did
they get here so fast? Sum 1 told them. Sum 1 set us up.

Jaden lookd at me. You no thats rite he said.
They were wating for us. They were reddy the hole
time. Wen we all got there they jumpd us.

Thats what Jello thinks said Snocone. I find out
who set us up Im going to kill him he said.

The bathroom had hi walls and his voys went *ping pong ping.*

Where is Jello? ast Jaden.

Snocone shook his head.

Sum 1 gave us up he said agane. Sum 1 told the cops about the deel.

1 of the Angels said Jaden. Or the yanks.

Not the yanks said Snocone. They wudnt tell the cops here.

Angels then.

Yah there the bad guys I said.

Mayb.

Being in the bathroom reminded me. I went over and peed. There were 4 places and I pickd the far 1.

What now? said Snocone. Cops going to pick us all up and sum 1 going to give us away agane. Going to work with the cops so he wont go to jale.

No way I said.

I was drying my hands.

Whos going to give us away? Not Jaden not me I said. Not you or Jello or Cobra or Beens or Morgan or even Xray. Were 15 I said. Together we fly. Rite?

They stared at me.

Sum thing my grampa told me I said.

Cops got Morgan said Snocone. I saw them. And they got Beens and Cobra and Xray in the parking lot. We'll never sell those guns now.

Guns? I said.

The deels dead said Snocone. Cops will catch us all. The only 1 wholl get out is the 1 who gave us away. The rat.

Guns? I said. They talkd sum more about a rat in the possy and about Jackfish and how the cops were probly there 2. I stared into the meer and thot about what was going on. Guns. Wow.

You dint do it did you Bunny? said Jaden. His face was all tite and twistd.

Huh?

You told Cobra that Al Capoli was in Jackfish. Scratch went up there and found him and so did the guys from Buffalo—and thats why there was a deel today. There wudnt be a deel without you. Did you tell the cops 2? Did you sell us out? He stood beside me. His eyes were big and sad in the meer. Mine were small and blank. I punchd myself in the meer. Nothing happend to the glass. My fist hurt.

Did you Bunny?

I shook my head.

Im 2 stupid I said.

We left Snocone in the bathroom. We went past a muffin place and a bikini place and an other close place.

I never new it was guns I said.

Huh?

The stuff in those boxes. Guns. I never new. The boxes said car parts. You said it was stuff. I dint no stuff ment guns.

Cobra found a hole stash of them he said. They were in a barn out in the country sum ware. Old ones but never bin used. He got them reel cheep from the lady who ownd the farm. Were selling them to the Angels and the Buffalo guys and there selling us stuff. Like a pool you no—they have drugs and money and we have guns. Evry 1 gets sum thing.

Drugs? I said. Like—drugs?

That was the problem with Al Capoli—he ran away with Rockos drugs. Cobra told me about it. Thats why there calling him a rat.

I was lost. I meen I new ware I was but I was lost 2.

So the cops r after us for selling drugs?

No—guns. The Buffalo guys had the drugs.

He shruggd.

I cant beleev your upset Bunny. Your a tuff guy. You have to be—you made it thru juvy. Your 1 of us. And—and—you killd sum 1. Whats rong with you?

No I dint.

What do you meen?

I dint kill any 1.

He grabbd my arm near Grampas tatoo. The tatoo I put goop on. The tatoo Id lookd at 100 times. 200. 1000 times.

See that candl he said. Its out. That meens a dead body.

It does?

You belong to the 15 Street possy and you killd sum 1. Thats what the tatoo meens. You killd sum 1 for the possy.

I shook my head.

No I dint.

Not now but wen you were in jale.

I wasnt in jale.

You said you were.

No—you said so.

You had to check in with your mom. Thats your prole offiser.

No I said. Its my mom.

We were in front of a place selling glasses. They were all over the windo—a store full of eyes staring out at us. Sum things began to make sens. The jale stuff yah and me being in the possy even tho I was white. And also the guns—*bang bang*. Jeez Bunny I thot how dum can you get? Cobra on the phone to Buffalo. Jaden thinking I was OK.

Hah.

Xept there was still lots I dint understand. Like why Grampas tatoo was the same as the possy tatoo or what I was doing here in the mall running away from the pleece with my best frend. Or if he was my best frend.

I new more than I used to and I still dint no any thing.

I startd to count the glasses in the shop windo.

Bunny said Jaden.

I kept counting.

You saying your not part of the possy? Come on he said. What about that tagging we did? And the fiting and driving round? Member what you said just now in the bathroom? *Together we fly.*

He grabbd me.

You got the ink Bunny. The cops r after you. What r you going to do?

20 21 22 I said.

What about you and me? Were frends rite? Rite?

I pulld away from him. I was way stronger.

I ran.

Hey Bunny—come back!

I dint.

I WAS—I DUNNO WHAT I WAS.

NUM I GESS. I breethd. The deel was guns and drugs and money. I was part of the possy. I was part of the deel. I breethd. In 2 3 4. I felt the gun in my pocket. I membered Jello giving me the gun and how cool that was. I meen guns r cool. You feel strong with a gun. There grate for killing zombis. But this gun was differnt. This was reel. Cops were after me cuz of guns. They were shooting there guns cuz I was selling guns. It was scary and confusing and bad. I breethd. My arm said I was part of the possy. Cobra said I was part of the possy. Jaden and Jello and Snocone and Beens were my frends.

But I dint belong. I dint kill any 1 or go to jale. So my arm was a liar and I was a liar and I wasnt part of the possy and the guys wernt my frends. Not even Jaden. I breethd and ran. In 2 3.

I herd yelling. Peepl were pointing at me. I had the gun in my hand. I droppd it and ran and then I thot—thats rong. I shud hide it. So I went back to ware it was spinning around on the floor and pickd it up and kept going til I came to the fountin and threw it in. But wen I lookd back I cud see it sitting there. It was huge—like a frying pan or sum thing. So I went into the fountin and grabbd it and put it back in my pocket and ran. I was running and dripping from the bottom of my pants and crying.

Yah crying. I wiped my eyes. I ran.

Close store. Shoo store. An other close store. TV store. I stoppd.

TVs were looking out so you cud watch them and peepl around me were saying wow and o my god and like that. The TVs were showing pick sures of the mall. There was the parking lot and the SUV and pleece car and bikes. There was the M pole. We were rite there a few minits ago. The news was about us. Across the bottom of the screen was a line of words.

GANG SHOOT OUT IN WEST TRONO MALL.

All the TVs had this. I saw it 4 5 7 8 times in the windo. I checkd each TV. Now they all showd pick sures of the pleece with sheelds and masks. And a guy lying on the ground.

Hey thats Bobby I said out loud and peepl turnd to look. Sum 1 pointd at my lying arm with the 15 and the candl. I dint no what els to do so I ran away with my wet pants flapping on my legs. Round the next bend I saw 2 pleece men in the distance and I held my gun over my head and ran tords them shouting help and hey and I give up but they got xited and took out there guns and pointd them at me. So I ran back the way I came past the TVs only this time I took a differnt turn and came to a store with paper on the windos so you cudnt see in. The paper said *COMING SOON* on it and the door was open a littl so I pushd on it and went in. The place was empty. I was alone and crying in an empty store. I countd my breths for a bit and took out my phone and calld Mom and Spencer. No anser. At the back of the store I found boxes like the kind washers and dryers come in. I threw my gun in 1 of them. And hid behind it wen the the door opend and the Angels came in.

Thats rite. Me behind the box and 3 Angels in the room. They dint talk much xept to sware. They wantd to no what went rong just like Snocone did. Sum 1 sold us down the river they said. Sum 1 from 15 Street talkd to the cops.

They used a word a lot. I wonderd if 1 of them was black and how he wud feel about that word. But probly they were all white.

I thot about me. I ran away so I wasnt in the possy any more and I dint like that. Drugs and guns were bad but so was being alone. Jaden used to be my frend. Man I dint like not having a frend.

The Angels were talking about a guy named Butch. Butch had the cash in a nap sack they said. Butch was pretty smart. He wud find a way to hide the cash from the cops and those basterds from 15 Street.

I dint like them calling 15 Street names and I must of made a noys. They herd it and came charjing back and found me. They were white guys all rite— with lether jackets and long stringy hair. 1 of them had a beerd like a patch on his chin. Wen they saw my tatoo they swore at me and said the possy had reckd evrything. Im not in the possy I said but they dint beleev me. They jumpd at me and the fite was on.

3 to 1 is tuff. I cot 1 guys foot and pushd him away. The other 2 were punching. I duckd 1 punch and cot the other 1. I got a kick in like Morgan had tot me and sum 1 went down. An other guy got me in the gut but not hard. I spun side ways and grabbd 1 guys rist and that hurt him. O he said. I ran for the door but sum 1 nockd me down from behind befor I got there. I got up and 2 guys were kicking me. I cot 1 foot and pushd it hi in the air and the guy fell but the other guy got me in the nee and I went down and then they were all round me kicking. That was bad. 1 of them had cowboy boots. I stoppd fiting and tryd to cover myself up. This went on for a wile and then I herd a voys I new.

Get away it said. Get away now or Ill shoot.

I lookd up.

I meen it. You basterds get the hell away from him.

It was Jaden. He stood in the doorway. He had his gun pointd at the Angels. Nun of them had guns— just Jaden. He was smaller than any 1 but the gun made a differnts. He held it in both hands. The end was reel still.

You wont shoot said the Angel with the patch beerd.

O yah? said Jaden.

You wont dare.

O yah?

He shot the box at the back. The Angels jumpd. Me 2—it was so loud and suprising. Jaden movd the gun back so that it was pointing at them agane.

I was standing up. My side hurt from the cowboy boots. Hi Jaden I said.

Hey Bunny.

I was mad at the Angels for hurting me and for being Angels and saying bad things about us. And I was happy to see Jaden. Mostly I was happy.

Come over here he said to me.

I did.

You OK?

Sure.

The Angel with the beerd said that if he shot any more the cops wud here him.

Im not scard of noys said Jaden. You were making noys wen you were beeting on Bunny. I herd you. Thats why Im here. It took all 3 of you eh? 3 big Angels to take 1 of the possy.

They dint say any thing.

Were going now. Let us alone. No 1 messes with 15 Street. Come on Bunny.

There was a bench out front of the COMING SOON store and we jammd it next to the door. Now the Angels cudnt get out for a wile.

We ran. I dint think about not staying with Jaden and he dint think of it ether.

Thanks I said.

Uh huh.

We kept going.

Wide you run away? he said. Was it about the guns?

I dint no how to xplane. Guns and drugs and my arm being a ly. Me being in the possy and then not in. Him and me being frends and then not being frends. I dint no.

It was all—evrything I said. It was evrything.

I wavd my hands round.

He nodded. It was quiet ware we were—no 1 was yelling. I cud hear music playing thru the mall. I new the song. Baby baby sum thing.

Guns arnt all bad said Jaden. Good thing I have 1 or youd still be getting kickd.

Yah I gess so I said.

We came to the fountin ware I got my pants wet. There was a bench and we sat down. Jaden told me about his mom then. She was in sum place a long way away and she was stacking time—48 months and she was haff way thru her stacking and that was why he was living with his gramma.

I dint understand about the stacking but I nodded.

I hate it at Grammas he said. She makes me dress up and go to church and she prays for me all the time. Cobra said I cud stay with him wen the deel went thru and he got a bigger place. Id have my own room and evrything. Xept now Cobras going to go to jale like Mom and Ill have to keep staying at Grammas.

He side. Its aw full.

I saw how much the guns ment. With the money from selling them the possy cud keep hanging out at the jim and Jello cud go on traning and Jaden cud live with his brother insted of his gramma. And now nun of this wud happen.

And stacking time ment being in jale. Thats ware Jadens mom was. No wonder he lookd sad.

I put my hand on his sholder. Its aw full at your grammas but it cud be worse.

Yah? How?

If they catch us now.

Yah he said. Then well go to jale 2. Yah that wud be worse.

The fountin stoppd. It does that sum times. I cud here the song going *ooo ooo ooo*.

I missd you Bunny he said. Wen you ran away.

Yah me 2.

Guns were bad rite? Xept that guns helpd my frends in the possy and Jadens gun saved me from the Angels. So guns were bad xept wen they wernt.

WE LOOK RONG
SAID JADEN.

YOUR TATOO AND MY rippd pants. We look
like we shudnt be here. Peepl r staring he said.

Can we change how we look? I said. I cud put my
hair differnt. And you cud—what?

He grabbd my hand.

What is it?

Your a jeenyus Bunny.

No Im not.

Come on he said. Sports store is rite here.

He pulld and I followd him. The fountin was
going agane. Im not a jeenyus I said.

Yes you r.

There were esclaters up and down. At the top of the esclaters we ran into the Angel with the gloves. He tryd to punch me. I twistd him round and he calld Jaden and me a name. Reely. First time I have ever bin calld that. Up close like this and without his helmet on I cud see his shiny haircut and I new who he was and why Jaden was so frowny at him.

No 1 messes with my frend I said.

He was facing the other way now so I twistd him sum more and he trippd and fell down the esclaters. He lay at the bottom for a second and then limpd off.

Thats 2 times you got him said Jaden.

On the back of his jacket he had the Angel tag and the name Butch.

Butch I thot. Did you here what he calld us? I ast.

Yes.

But me 2. He calld me 1. Does that meen Im a brother now?

Jaden laffd and pushd me into the store. It felt good to here him laff. And to not be alone.

The store peepl stood by the windo looking out. The close were in piles. I grabbd a shirt and pants and then thot—a hat. The changing room had 4 hooks on the wall. I countd them and then agane. 4.

I put on the new close and left my old 1s on the hooks. I checkd in the meer. Was that me? Yah. I made a face. Yah. I pulld up the sleevs and then put them down agane. I dint like the long sleevs but cops were looking for a tatoo.

My phone rang from my pocket on the hook. It was Mom.

Bunny? Ware r you? she ast but she dint let me anser. Im at the phone store and they gave me a new phone number she said. I cant keep my old 1. So now you have the number rite? Its on your phone.

O I said. Rite.

Stay in touch she said. Dont lose this new number.

I thot about telling her what was going on but I dint no ware to start. I memberd I was sposd to be close to home and not at the mall. And then she was gone.

I put the phone in my pocket.

Nock on the change room door. I opend and it was a store girl. She walkd rite in.

That looks grate Bunny she said. Differnt. The long sleev. The hat is grate 2. Good for you.

She smiled at me. I dint no how she new my name.

Well what do you think? she ast.

I shook my head. I dint no what she was talking about.

Dont you reconize me?

And then I saw. Your—

I stoppd and startd agane.

R you? I said.

YES SHE SAID

IM JADEN. AND SHE WAS—I cud here it.
She sounded like Jaden. But she lookd like a girl.
She was Jaden in girl close.

Wow I said.

Good disguys huh?

Yah.

Her top was blu and white stripes. Her skirt and
nee sox were blu too. I gess I shudnt be saying her—
Jaden was still a guy. A guy in a skirt. His skirt was
blu. His.

What r you doing now?

He had his folding nife out. He cut the plastic tags off my close. He had to rip the end of my shirt but it tuckd into the pants and you cudnt see any thing rong.

Dont want the alarm to go off wen we get out of the store do we? he said.

Uh I said.

He put the nife in a pocket of his skirt and stood next to me so there we were in the meer. He pushd his hair around to make it stand up more.

You look funny I said.

Shut up.

The sports store had stuff for camping and swimming and running round. The models all had arms and legs but no heads. Funny eh? A lady lookd like she was playing tennis but had no head. How did she no ware the ball was? The sines said *SUMMER SALE!!* and *50% OFF!!* and like that. We went down stares past a seen with a tent and campfire and kids and mom and dad. I stoppd to stare. The trees had leevs. Mom had a nap sack. The fire was flicking and evrything. It was so reel. But the only 1 who had a head was the deer in the background. Jaden told me to come on.

There rosting weenees I said. How r they going to eat them with no heads?

Thats wen we herd the shots. 1 2. Then a screem. We ran out into the mall and there were sum more screems and an other shot. Peepl came out of the stores asking did you here? We were up stares and we lookd down over the raling and lissend to the sound of the shots getting softer like at the loyers offics that time.

Bang-ang-ang. Bang-ang-ang.

A guy ran up in those thick shoos for old peepl. He wasnt old but his shoos were. He had his name on his shirt. *Dave*. There shooting *Dave* said. Pleece and gangs shooting each other. They shot my boss in the store.

Dave ran away and we went after him—me and Jaden and evry 1 els. Wen we got to the movy theeter the peepl wating in line saw us running and came over to run with us so now there were lots of us running. The girl next to me was spilling her bag of popcorn—evry step she wud spill sum more. We ran until we herd shots from in front of us and then we stoppd and ran back the way we came. You no those birds that fly all over the sky together? Like that.

We ran back to the movy theeter and stoppd agane. A line of blu was coming tords us. Cops. Lots of them. We watchd them go into 1 place and come out agane and go into the next place closer to us. They were serching the mall.

What do we do? Jaden ast me. What do we do Bunny? We cant run any ware now.

We can see a movy I said.

I meen there we were.

Jaden pulld me past the soft loopy rope. No 1 was taking tickets. We ran past the booth and down the hall to the first door. Jaden was in front. He lookd weerd in girl close.

NIKKI THE COP CAME BACK

INTO THE ROOM WARE I was riting. She had a man with her. She calld him boss and told him who I was. He had those things that hold up your pants. What r they? Any way he had them. His shoos were shiny.

He leend on the table ware I was riting and crossd his arms.

Sarjent Nolan says your working hard son he said. Riting out what happend this afternoon r you?

Yes I said.

He nodded and said sum thing I dint hear. My ears were still ringing a bit. I ast him to say it agane.

We need your help son he said pretty loud.

Did you lose sum thing? I ast.

What?

My mom needs my help wen she loses stuff. I'm good at finding things.

He lookd over at Sarjent Nikki. She shruggd. Then back to me.

Yah I lost sum thing he said. I lost my key witness. He was working for us and now hes dying. You no who Im talking about son?

I shook my head.

Yes you do. You were there wen it happend.

He frownd down at me. Big thumbs behind his spenders. The lite over the door had a cage round it like a hocky mask. I dint see that til now.

I want you to be my witness son he said. I want you to ID sum bad guys for me. Can you do that?

ID? Like who they r?

Yes son. That's xactly rite. Who they r. I want you to take Jacksons place. He was working for us and now I want you to. I need sum 1 to put in jale and I need a witness to help me.

O I said.

It was still tuff to think about Jackson.

You sure you dont want me to find sum thing? I ast. A pen or sum keys? Moms always losing her car keys.

Sarjent Nikki and her boss went into a corner and talkd for a moment. I cudnt here what they said but I new they were talking about me and not being happy.

❖

Mary Lee Berdit felt the same way about me. We were both in the class play in Grade 4. She was the lady and and I was the prints and in the big seen I had to skip over and kiss her. I was the prints cuz nun of the other guys wantd to be. We did the seen over and over and I kept getting it rong—ether the skip or the kiss. I must of kissd Mary Lee 10 times and thats a lot of kissing. Finally she neeld down and told the teecher we had to stop now. She slappd her hand on the stage and said I was recking the play. The teecher was OK. She smiled at me and said she wud try to think of a way to make it easy for me. No 1 els in the class wud look at me. Ed and them laffd and startd to hit each other with there card bord sords. I stood in the middl of the stage in my cape and boots and countd the folds in the curtins.

✤

Boss was mad at me just like Mary Lee. Id messd up his plans. He and Nikki talkd about Jackson who was mayb dying in hospital. All they had was me and I was no good. He left without saying good by and Sarj Nikki took me to see Mom. She was in a wating room with a worry face and a sell phone. She ast if I was dun yet. I said I was still riting. She shook her head and said O Bunny. She said that a bunch of times all reddy. O Bunny.

There was a form. Mom sined it fast and jerky like she had all the other forms.

Your helping them rite Bunny? she said. Your ansering what they ast you and telling them what happend.

Im trying I said.

Nikki took Mom aside and talkd for a minit or 2.

R you sure? said Mom. All rite. Ill make a call.

I still think its all a big mistake she said. Bunny dint no what he was doing. You dont no any thing do you Bunny?

I no lots of things I said.

No you dont! she yelld. No you dont!

I ast Nikki who Mom was going to call.

A loyer she said.

For me?

For you.

We were back in the riting room. She stared down at the table with my pile of yello paper.

You almost finishd?

Uh I said.

Well get going.

✽

Show nite and the jim was full of moms and dads. It was time for the big seen. Mary Lee put out her hand for a handshake. This was the teechers idea— so I wudnt get the kiss rong. I dint mind. I skippd across the stage with my hand out—only I trippd on my big prints boots and fell face down. O it hurt. Mary Lee screemd. There was blud from my nose all over the floor and my shirt. They pulld the curtin and evry 1 clappd.

You never forget stuff like that do you?

WE SAT

IN THE MIDDL OF THE THEETER. It was dark and loud. Jaden pulld me along an empty row and we sat down. The movy was at an xiting part. The guy in the movy ran across a bisy street and just missd getting hit by a truck. He ran thru a parking lot and down a lane. He climed a fence. He had a flappy white coat and a cut under his eye and his breth came fast. The music was the kind that goes *deedeedeedeedeedeedee* and makes you bite down hard.

Jaden leend over and ast if I herd sum thing.

What?

Sum thing outside?

No.

The movy playd. The bad guys after the guy in the white coat. They shoutd at him. The music got louder. The guy ran down stares and onto the subway and the doors closed and he got away. Then it was the next day and he was having coffee in his apartment. He still had the littl cut on his cheek from last nite but it lookd OK in fact it lookd pretty good. His hair was wet from the shower. Nice music so you new nothing bad wud happen.

Jaden wisperd what now?

I dont no. We missd the start of the movy.

I meen what about us?

O.

The guy with the cut went to anser the door bell and there were the bad guys agane—what a twist. They had there guns out and evrything.

O no I wisperd.

Jaden turnd in his seat. Behind us there were 2 lites from flashlites. They were moving down the theeter row by row. Pleece offisers—I cud see there hats. They were getting closer. I herd them wispering.

Clear they said. Clear.

O crap.

They were coming to our row next. I thot about all the running me and Jaden had dun today. Now there was no ware to run and no ware to hide. The pleece wud see our faces in a minit.

Jaden leend forward.

Hold me he wisperd.

What?

Its just pretend. Come on Bunny.

What?

And he put his arms round my neck and held on tite and kept his face close to my neck. And we sat there close to each other in the movy like we were— you no.

Ew.

I cudnt see the movy now but there was lots of yelling. The music was spiky—*CRAK! PONKA! SKIK! PONKA PONKA!* Sort of.

Relax wisperd Jaden.

His breth was in my ear. It was so weerd.

Ware r they? I ast.

Shhh. Dont talk.

But I want to—

He pulld my face down. With his lips on mine I cudnt talk. Im stronger than him so youd think

I cud pull away but he rappd his arms round me and hung on and I cudnt do it. I cudnt pull away.

Mm I said.

Mm he said.

And we were kind of kissing and I wantd to get away xept the pleece offisers were rite there with there flash lites. And the movy was going on. And evrything.

I countd in 2 3 4 out 2 3 4. I had to breeth thru my nose cuz my mouth was bisy. My eyes were closd. I herd the cops laffing and saying geez and look at those 2. And clear.

And I new sum thing about Jaden.

We kept kissing until the shooting startd.

IN THE MOVY

THE BAD GUYS WERE SHOOTING at the guy
with the cut face. And a few rows down from us
a guy in a lether jacket was running to the front and
the pleece were telling him to stop or they wud shoot
and he dint stop and there was a brite yello flash and
a boom and that was the pleece shooting. The guy
duckd and there was a flash and he was shooting
back. And there was an other flash from over on the
left and an other 1 from down at the front and sum
thing went past my head. There was yelling and more
shooting in the theeter and on the screen and I cudnt
here hardly any thing. And then the lites came up

and the room was full of smoke and it smelld like matches or no like fire cracks at the cottage. I wonder if weel do it next year? Probly not. But thats what it smelld like after the shooting. The start of summer. Pleece stood at the back and at the front with there guns out and there mouths open shouting. Guys lay on the floor with more pleece standing over them. Peepl peeping over the back of there chairs.

I was counting. 4 5 6 7. Freckls on Jadens face. I never thot of freckls on black faces but Jaden had sum and I was counting them. For head. Cheek. 8 9 10 11 12 13. Jadens lips were moving. I cudnt here. Littl dot freckls like with a pin. Other cheek. 13 14 15.

The movy stoppd. I lost count and startd agane. My ears got better. We marchd out of the theeter with our hands up. There were sum old peepl and they cudnt keep there hands up but the pleece said they were OK with there hands down. We all got in a line and walkd up the ramp and out the door and past the velvet ropes and there were more pleece standing there. Peepl were crying and shaking.

Wares your hat?

Jaden had to ast 2 times befor I herd.

I shook my head.

Did you see the dead guy? The Angel? You no who it was?

I shook my head agane. I was looking at Jadens shoos. They were the same 1s from this morning. From yesterday. The same shoos but Jaden was differnt.

The pleece kept us in line. 1 by 1. We walkd slow past the place ware they sell movy tickets—booth I meen. The door of the booth was open and there were pleece on both sides of the door and a curtin. We all walkd past.

Wen I got to the booth the pleece told me to stop. A pleece man pointd his gun at me and told me to step away from the line. He ast me my name and I told him. He ast me to pull up my sleev and I did. Jaden turnd round to look at me. So did sum of the others who were past the booth. An old lady ast what was behind the curtin. She ast a few times.

R you part of the 15 Street Possy? the cop ast me.
Uh I said.

I want to see! said the lady. I want to see!

She came out of the line and went rite up to the curtin talking all the time. Her voys was shaky like a yo yo or a pudding. I new who she was now—

the oldy from the bus on the way in. Dinty. She pulld away the curtin with her spider hands. And no 1 stoppd her cuz she was old I gess and cuz they were suprised and cuz they were looking at me.

There was a guy I new behind the curtin. I said hi. His pink shirt was dark under his arms. His mouth hung open. He lookd tired to deth. He nodded hi back at me.

You no this guy Jackson? ast the cop who was pointing his gun at me.

Your name is Jackson? I said to him.

Yah.

Jello Jackson?

He side.

Yah Bunny.

O.

A pleece woman was trying to drag Dinty out of the way and Dinty was fiting her—stomping down on her boot and throwing her arms round. I wonderd ware the bully with the red cap was. Mayb she was inside the theeter. Mayb she was shot along with the Angel. Dinty was calling the pleece woman a not see and peepl were staring.

The pleece man said I was under arrest.

I was thinking back. In Snocones basment wen the guys shoutd Jackson. In the pleece car that time wen the guy in the front ast if my name was Jackson. Jackson is a frend of ours he said and the other cop told him to shut up.

He was talking about Jello.

All this time Jello was like a statu. Black and smooth and no xpreshun. His hands were at his sides. His mouth was strate across like a bar in his fat face.

My pleece man told me to get down on the floor now. Dinty nockd the pleece woman in the chin with the back of her head. The cop trippd and fell forward and Dinty broke free. And now here was Jaden running rite at Jello and pulling out a gun. I movd without thinking without stopping without any thing. Jello and I grabbd Jadens hand at the same time so 3 of us were holding the gun at wunce. I dont no who pulld the trigger. The first bullet went into the air and hit sum kind of lite thing witch xploded into sparks. Jello got free for a second and I trippd him and we all went down rolling over and over and nocking into Dinty and the pleece woman and they fell 2. So all of us were tangld on the floor by the ticket booth. Jaden was yelling at Jello calling him a rat and saying he sold us out. Dinty was in between me and Jello but I wasnt worryd about her or the pleece woman who ended up under evry 1. I was fiting for the gun. I was scared that Jaden wud shoot Jello and I was scared that Jello wud shoot Jaden. I was more scared of that than any thing.

I wantd to ast Jello—did you reely sell us out? Were you on the phone to the cops in the parking lot? Is that why they got there so fast? And I wantd to ast—why?

But the hole fite only lastd a few more seconds and there wasnt time to ast him any thing. What happend was I pushd Jellos hand away from him and Dinty got hold of him under the arm and he got ticklish and let go of Jaden. And Jaden brot the gun down so it was aming at Jellos belly. I grabbd it just befor it went off.

The shot was softer than the others. Sort of a *plop* sound.

We were messd together on the floor—me and Jaden and Jello and the old lady and the pleece woman. Jadens face was next to mine.

Jello dint no you wen you walkd past I said.

No.

No 1 nose who you r I said. They no me but not you. You can get away.

The gun Jaden said.

I have the gun I said.

I shot Jello.

Did you? I said.

I dont no what happend. Its all a blur.

I WAS DUN. I DINT WANT TO RITE ANY THING EVER AGANE

AND IT WAS LATE like mid nite. Sarjent Nikki took my yello sheets of blobby riting to her desk to reed. I went to the bathroom with a pleece man wating outside. Wen I got back to the room Mom was there with a loyer for me. Not Jadens uncle who dint want me to tell him any thing. This was Grampas loyer from way back wen we all went to his offis. I new him rite away—his soot and smooth hair. He said hello Bernard and we had a talk him and me and Mom.

Things were seeryus he said. The pleece new I was in a gang and we were deeling guns and drugs with other gangs and there was shooting at the mall

194

and that I was part of that. He xplaned about Jello being a rat only he calld him a pleece inform ant. Now Jello was in hospital and mayb dying from being shot and they cudnt use him as a witness. And it was my falt. If he did dy the pleece were going to charj me with killing him. Not murder but sum loyer thing—sum thing about an axident and a killing.

I thot about Snocone in the bathroom at the mall wondering who gave us away. Jello. Huh. It was still hard to beleev. Mom said they cudnt put me in jale— that I was 2 much of a dummy. She dint say that but its what she ment.

You no him John! she said to the loyer. He dint no what he was doing!

The loyer shook his head and said the pleece were talking differnt. I wud go to jale unless I cud ID sum 1 who new about the guns. And I had to see the gun deel myself—I cudnt just here about it.

He said they wantd me to look at a line up. Wud I do that? I said sure. So a pleece woman took me and the loyer to a dark room with 1 wall that was all windos looking into the next room. 5 guys walkd into that room and stood on the wall.

Its 1 way glass the pleece woman told me. You can see them but they cant see you. Dont be scared.

Why wud I be scared? I said.

There were numbers sprayd on the wall. 1 2 3 4 5. They stood under the numbers. The pleece woman pushd a button and talkd to them. Number 1 step forward she said. Turn left. Turn rite. Walk back. Then Number 2 and Number 3 and Number 4 and Number 5. And they went back to standing.

The pleece woman ast if I new the guys.

Yes I said. Xept for Number 4.

You ID them.

You meen who they r?

Yes. There in the 15 Street Possy?

Yes I said. Xept for Number 4.

So Number 1 2 3 and 5 belong to the possy?

Yes.

And what r there names?

I told her. Snocone was there and Cobra and Xray and Bonesaw. She rote down the names. It was weerd but nice to see the guys. Cobra was as tall as ever. The next tallest guy was Bonesaw and he only came up to Cobras sholder.

The pleece woman told Number 4 he cud go. Now it was only the guys I new. She ast if I new there reel names and I shook my head and she told me to say no so the tape recorder cud here me.

No I said. And then I said—O wate.

Snocones reel name is Arthur I said.

We went back to the room and wated and Sarjent Nikki came in looking tired. Her boss was mad. Sure Way Mall was all over the news. They were calling it a war zone and blaming the pleece for letting it happen. That was bad enuff but what was worse was the pleece cudnt put any 1 in jale for what happend. Not for long any way. They found sum guns and sum bags of white powder but no proof of a deel.

We dint even find any money she said.

Mom was shaking her head. A war zone she wisperd. O Bunny!

We need sum 1 to say that Jeffers and Mcray were deeling guns said Nikki. We dont want them to get away with a littl charj like having fire arms. We want to put them in jale for years and for that to happen we need a witness—sum 1 who saw them. Do you no what I meen?

I shook my head.

Who r Jeffers and Mcray? I ast.

You no them as Cobra and uh Bonesaw.

O I said.

You no sum 1 named Cobra? said Mom.

Sure. Hes OK.

Mom put her hand to her mouth.

Your new in the possy said Sarjent Nikki. And your not like the rest of them. We dont want you in jale—we want the others. You pickd them out of the line up Bunny. Now we need you tell us what you saw them do. And it has to be better than your report here.

She wavd the yello papers around. Turnd out that what I rote was no good. Funny after the ours of riting and my sore hand and evrything. The pleece cudnt use what I rote cuz I dint see any 1 by guns or sell guns. Or drugs. Jaden told me there were guns in the boxes but I dint see them myself.

Its 2 bad Bunny said the sarjent. We had hopes for you.

The loyer jumpd in here and said sum thing about me trying. Sum thing sum thing good faith. Nikki came back with sum thing els. Sum thing missing. Or mayb my report was missing. Mom watchd back and forth.

Want to no sum thing? I wasnt upset about the report. I was even kind of glad. I dint want the possy to go to jale cuz of me. Guns were bad and all but was the possy bad? I dint think so. I liked them. They were on my side. Witch made them the good guys. Mayb not Jello. He was a rat. Mayb he was bad.

Her boss wantd to put me in jale said Nikki. But there mite be a way to save myself if I cud tell the pleece more about Jaden.

Whos Jaden? Mom ast me.

My frend I said. I told you about Jaden.

Hes a gang member said Sarjent Nikki. Mom got up and walkd away shaking her head. The sarjent sat on the table next to me with her feet hanging. Frendly you no? She pattd the yello papers.

You rote about this storaj locker down by the Lake Shore she said. You got the guns and loded them into the car. Jaden new the way there and had a key and you went with him. So you cud be a witness about that. The only problem is that we dont no much about Jaden. We dont no ware he lives or what he looks like. We dont no ware he mite be hiding out. Hes disappeared.

Uh I said.

Wud you sit down with a pleece artist and help us make a pick sure of Jaden?

Im pretty stupid I said.

Do you now ware Jaden is now?

No.

If you told us ware Jaden was now—thatd be helping. My boss wud like that. Do you understand Bunny?

She leend close. Her eyes near mine. Her frown. Her belt holding up her uniform pants.

Can you tell us any thing about Jaden that wud help us locate him?

I new sum thing all rite. But I cudnt tell.

Uh I said.

Thats 2 bad Bunny she said. That reely is 2 bad.

❉

The loyer went off to talk with Sarjent Nikki. Mom ast how I was feeling. I told her my ears were better but my hand was killing me. Your arm? she ast and I said no my hand from riting. My arm is fine.

I blame that tatoo said Mom. Your grampa and that stupid will of his! You were a norml happy boy last week. And now look at you! This is a nite mare. Your a criminal. Your dad and I r very unhappy.

She stood there and side for a bit.

I ast her how you new sum thing. I was thinking about Jaden.

What do you meen Bunny?

Isnt that what you teech at skool Mom? You teech about noing things. Spencer said so. Im stupid but can you xplane it to me? About noing? Cuz I no sum thing and I dont no how I no it. I just do.

Mom stared at me like she had never seen me befor. Like I was a stranger.

The loyer came back with a long face. He talkd to Mom for a bit and she startd crying. I cud go home and get sum things but I had to come back to the pleece stashun and stay over nite. Like a sleep over I said. Mom cryd sum more.

The loyer took me home. He was in charj of me. We walkd down the hall of the pleece stashun side by side. I had my yello sheets of riting since the pleece cudnt use them. I folded them up and put them in my pocket. The loyer ast me how I thot Grampa wud feel rite now. Your grampa was so proud of you boys he said. He wantd so much for you.

He wantd you all to have xiting ventures and lern things about your selves. Wud your grampa be happy with you now Bernard? he ast.

I think so.

How can you say that? Your in pleece hands. A boy mite dy.

Bad things happen I said. Grampa new that. He droppd boms.

The loyer shut his mouth.

We went out the back door to the parking lot ware the loyer had his car. It was nite time and the street lites were on. The air smelld good after all those ours inside. Gess who was getting out of a pleece car as I walkd past.

Can you gess?

We stared at each other. Her lips movd but there was no sound. Help me she said. I cud count the seconds ticking 1 2 3 4 5.

1. I thot about Sarjent Nikki wondering ware Jaden was. The pleece dint no about Jaden. They dint no who this was getting out of the car.

2. I thot about Grampas letter. The tatoo was so I wud no I had a crew behind me. He wantd me to no I had frends.

3. I thot about the first time Jaden smiled at me. And all the other times.

4. I thot about kissing her and finding out she was a girl like Mary Lee was a girl. I new it the way I new water was wet. I just new it.

5. I thot about her saying help me.

That was all the thinking I had time for. Next thing I new Jaden was running past me out of the parking lot and onto the street and the pleece man was running after her. He dint get far cuz I put my foot out and he trippd over it. He grabbd me and we went down. Forget falling like a ball—the pleece man was on top of me. I fell like a brick and hit my head. I saw stars.

THAT WAS A LONG TIME AGO

LIKE MONTHS AND MONTHS. My head got better. Jello dint dy from the gun shot but he got sick and dyed in hospital and I went to jale. Im still here. Its not so bad. Theres a jim and a TV room and a caff. The foods OK. The wire fence is hi but I can see thru it to the street and the houses and peepl walking by. The 3 guys in my room were OK after the first nite. They saw the tatoo and Benj said holy crap. Next day he brot me xtra brekfast. And the next day. I had to tell him OK enuff. Moms stoppd crying wen she comes to visit. Summer went by and fall. Im in skool—Grade 9. Im fixing up my pleece report to hand in as a riting project. My teecher saw sum of it all reddy. He said O.

✦

Jaden came to visit the first Sunday after I got here. She wore a green dress with buttons and had her hair pulld back and lookd pretty. She was a girl all the time now in case the pleece were looking for the boy Jaden. She said I cud call her Jade. The visitors room was mostly moms and mostly sad. But I wasnt sad and nether was Jade.

She told me what happend to her that day. How she foold the pleece pretending to be so freakd out by the shooting that she wudnt talk not even to say her name. She dint want them taking her home and finding she was Cobras sister. They took her to a crazy hospital and were nice to her for ours. And wen she still wudnt say any thing they took her back to the pleece stashun to be a missing person—witch is wen she saw me and took a chance on running.

Wow I said. And how did you no I wud help?

I dint she said. But I new you were on my side. I was hoping.

Wen I told her ware the money was she opend
her mouth wide and said r you sure? And I said no.
But that wen I was hiding in the COMING SOON
store I herd the Angels talking about Butch and
the money—and that wen I threw Butch down the
esclater he dint have a nap sack but that the headless
mom in the camp fire seen did.

So you think Butch hid the money in the sport
store so the cops wudnt find it on him?

Mayb I said.

And he cant get it now. I wonder if he told
any 1 about it befor he got shot? Ha! You reely r a
jeenyus Bunny.

No. But Ive always bin good at finding things
I said.

Jade gave me a hug on her way out and Greg went
woo-hoo. Greg is OK for a gard. Next time she came
she told me about wating in the sports store til
no 1 was looking and grabbing the nap sack off the
headless mom. Jade comes here a lot—most Sundays
even tho its a trane ride for her. We walk round
outside if its sunny.

We talkd about Jello 1 time. She dint no why
he turnd into a rat. He was in jale befor she said.

Mayb the cops had sum thing on him. Said she dint care. A rats a rat she said.

Last time she came was weerd cuz Mom and Dad and Spencer came 2. They walkd in the visiting room wen Jade was all reddy there and we were kind of holding hands. Mom stoppd in the doorway and the other 2 bumpd into her.

Wen Jade left Mom was super polite like how very nice to meet you. Dad pointd his finger at her and said see ya later. I thot Spencer wud never be able to close his mouth it was open so wide.

Bun man he said.

Yah I no.

❋

Scratch came to visit last Sunday. I dint no him til he told me his name. Hes a tuff littl guy with pointy shoos and a jacket. He wantd to see my tatoo. Then he nodded and said—I thot so.

What?

Thats mine he said. You got my tatoo.

My grampa—

It was a mistake he said.

He took off his jacket and opend his shirt. On the back of his sholder he had a tatoo of a bug smoking a cigar. Under the bug pick sure was sum riting—*Together we fly.* Grampas motto from back in the war.

I was next after you at the place on Lake Shore said Scratch. I dint see the ink til it was dun. Then I almost killd that dorf. She blamed Billy—said it was him bying the place in a rush and getting the orders rong. And she said you dint no any better—that you thot you were getting the rite ink.

So Scratch had my tatoo and I had his.

Im used to it now he said. I dont check back there very much and wen I do its pretty good.

He pointd at my arm. That says you belong to the 15 Street Possy and you killd sum 1 he said.

I no I said. Im a fake.

But r you? he ast. Dint you kill 1 of 15s enemys? Jackson was a rat and you helpd the possy by getting rid of him.

I said I dint reely do it.

You were there wen it happend. Your in jale for it. Cobra and Xray and Morgan r out now but your still behind a fence. I think you ernd the tatoo Bunny.

Funny the way he put it. It almost made sens.

Greg the gard came over and ast Scratch to do up his shirt. Do you mind? he said and Scratch said not at all. I ate a cooky. The caff puts them out on Sundays. I thot of the things that had happend cuz of my tatoo. The guys I new. The things I did. The things I was doing and wud do. I thot about Grampa agane. With his hat and his jokes and his arms on my sholders saying Dont be sorry for yourself.

Well I wasnt. For all that went rong I wasnt sorry for me.

Scratch ast wen I was getting out. Sum time in June I said. The sentens was a year less a day. My mom has it ritten down I said.

He said they missd me down at the jim. Morgan and them. The money in the nap sack was paying the rent with enuff left over for Cobras new place. Jade dint come round very much he said.

You new about her I said.

About—?

About Jaden being a girl.

He shook his head.

Cobra and the gramma were the only 1s who new he said. And then you.

Wen Scratch left I got my coat and walkd around the fence. I thot of Grampa holding the sord and saying I wud no who the good guys were wen the time came. Trust yourself he said. Benj came out and walkd with me. He had a cupl cookys and gave me 1. We talkd about hocky. He liked the Leefs. They were his teem. There going to win tonite he said.

How do you no that?

I dont he said. But Im hoping.

ACKNOWLEDGMENTS

This book wouldn't have got started without Eric Walters's big idea. And it wouldn't have got plotted without the input of the other six authors in the series. Particular thanks to my series brother, Ted Staunton. Content and spelling help was provided by my children and my MFA class at Guelph-Humber. Thanks, guys. John Cusick and Scott Treimel did their usual stellar agenting. And I want to acknowledge a huge debt of thanks to the incomparably generous, gracious and flexible Sarah Harvey, series editor. Sorry for the gray hairs!

RICHARD SCRIMGER is the award-winning author of more than fifteen books for children and adults. His books have been translated into Dutch, French, German, Thai, Korean, Portuguese, Slovenian, Italian and Polish. The father of four children, he has written humorous pieces about his family life for *The Globe and Mail* and *Chatelaine*. Visit Richard at www.scrimger.ca.